About

David Quantick writes for television (*Veep, The Thick of It, Brass Eye*) and radio (*One, The Blagger's Guide*). He is also the author of the comic novel *Sparks* (described as 'excellent' by Neil Gaiman), the comic book *That's Because You're A Robot* and several short films, including the award-winning *Welcome to Oxmouth*. A scriptwriter, broadcaster and comedy writer, David once appeared on *Celebrity Come Dine With Me*, where he came fifth out of five.

GO WEST

GO WEST

GO WEST

DAVID QUANTICK

Unbound Digital

This edition first published in 2018

Unbound

6th Floor Mutual House, 70 Conduit Street, London W1S 2GF

www.unbound.com

ISBN (eBook): 978-1-912618-71-2

ISBN (Paperback): 978-1-912618-70-5

Design by Mecob

Printed and bound in Great Britain by Clays Ltd, Elcograf S.p.A.

MIX
Paper from
responsible sources
FSC® C018072

To Dad

Dear Reader,

The book you are holding came about in a rather different way to most others. It was funded directly by readers through a new website: Unbound.

Unbound is the creation of three writers. We started the company because we believed there had to be a better deal for both writers and readers. On the Unbound website, authors share the ideas for the books they want to write directly with readers. If enough of you support the book by pledging for it in advance, we produce a beautifully bound special subscribers' edition and distribute a regular edition and e-book wherever books are sold, in shops and online.

This new way of publishing is actually a very old idea (Samuel Johnson funded his dictionary this way). We're just using the internet to build each writer a network of patrons. Here, at the back of this book, you'll find the names of all the people who made it happen.

Publishing in this way means readers are no longer just passive consumers of the books they buy, and authors are free to write the books they really want. They get a much fairer return too – half the profits their books generate, rather than a tiny percentage of the cover price.

If you're not yet a subscriber, we hope that you'll want to join our publishing revolution and have your name listed in one of our books in the future. To get you started, here is a £5 discount on your first pledge. Just visit unbound.com, make your pledge and type BREAD19 in the promo code box when you check out.

Thank you for your support,

Dan, Justin and John
Founders, Unbound

Super Patrons

Sue & Steve, Alf & Pat
Moose Allain
Gus Alvarez
Judith Anderson
Jamie Anderson
Cam Baddeley
Stuart Bailie
Matthew Bate
Bob Beaupre
Meat Bingo
Will Birch
Paul Bloomfield
Iain Bonehill
Richard Boon
Stuart Boutell
Stuart Brooks
Guy Brown
Peter Bulloch
Kate Bulpitt
Ali Burns
Adrian Burns
Amanda Busby
Ian Caine
Martin Carr
David Catley
Auntie Ceri
Alison J Clark
Emma Clarke
John Cody
Jonathan Coe
Stevyn Colgan
Darren Corcoran

Andy Cragg
John Crawford
Anthony Critchlow
Peter Curran
Johnny Daukes
Nick Davey
Mat Davies
Geoff Deane
Stephen Delaney
Anna Dent
Steve Doherty
Jemima Dury
Barbara Ellen
Linda Marric & Zack Evans
Simon Everett
Mike Finney
Patrick Fitzgerald
Joe Fowler
Bill Freedman
Jim Galbraith
Sophie Goldsworthy
Kenneth Gordon
Ken Gorry
Esther Green
Tony Hannan
Donna Harle
Juliet Harris
Sue Harris
Anna Harrison
Ian Hartley
Jason Hazeley
Lesley Hoyles
Maxim Jakubowski
Mike James
Peter Jaques
Paul Jaunzems

Gary Jones
Dan Kieran
Peter King
Michele Kirsch
Elizabeth Knight
Michaela Knowles
Michael Knowles
Julia Koenig
Jenny Landreth
Mick Lemmerman
Stephen Lennon
Justin Lewis
Geoff Lloyd
Kathy Loizou
Graham Lovatt
Calum Macaulay
Yvonne Maddox
Nick Madge
Annie Mannion
The Margate Bookie
Andy Martin
Ian Martin
Polly Fiona McDonald
John A C McGowan
Chris McLaren
Tony McMahon
Wendy McQueen
Craig Melvin
Roger Miles
Chris Miller
Peter Miller
John Mitchinson
J Moe
Arsalan Mohammad
Dave Morley
Julia Morris

Sarah Morris
Greg Muden
Bruno Noble
Mark O'Neill
Coral Rubble & Sandy Overlay
Scott Pack
Michael Paley
Lev Parikian
Lesley Pearson
Jerry Perkins
Steve Perrin
Dan Peters
Grant Philpott
Michael Quantick
Sheila Quantick
Duncan Raggett
Leslie Ramage
Slam Raman
Lucian Randall
Karen Reed
Gillian Reynolds
Emma Richardson
Christopher Richardson
Glenn Richer
Claire Ridall
Tony Roche
Geraint Rogers
Catherine Rosenthal
Alison Ross
Tim Saxton
Irfan Shah
Carl Shanahan
Gary Sharp
Dale Shaw
Tamsin Shelton
David Simpkin

Eric Sinclair
Jan Skakle
Keith Sleight
Nicholas Snowdon
Teresa Squires
Tracey Stevens
Bill Stone
Helen Stone
Matthew Sweet
Tot Taylor
Richard Thomas
Andy Thompson
Mike Scott Thomson
Ghislaine Tibbs
Matt Tiller
Alison Townley
David G Tubby
Rita Tweeter
Martyn Waites
Alex Walsh Atkins
Matthew Wasley
Nigel Wassell
Simon Watkins
Richie Webb
Jonathan Westwood
Ann Elizabeth White
Sam White
Wendalynn Wordsmith

Part One

'I can never feel all the nice things that have been said about *The Young Visiters* are really due to me at all, but to a Daisy Ashford of so long ago that she seems almost another person.'
– Daisy Ashford

CHAPTER ONE

'If, for example, a report casts doubt on a Rembrandt attribution because tests reveal a pigment only developed after the artist's death, contracts prevent the report's author from speaking out if that information is suppressed.'
– *The Guardian*, 22 February 2014

My name is Charlie Bread. I'm driving a red Jaguar Mark 2, I've got John Peel on the car stereo, and I'm going to Devon.

'Well, tonight,' says Peel, *'we return in the company of Viv Stanshall to Rawlinson End. This episode, number thirty-seven, is called Cabbage Looking In Mufti, don't ask me why. Before that, records from Lee Perry, David Bowie, The Waitresses, 999, Snatch, Bryan Ferry, Culture, The Ramones, Clash, Siouxsie and the Banshees – and The Stranglers.'*

I work for a major auction house – well, not as major as the two you've definitely heard of, Sotheby's and the other one, but Pring's is a close third to them – and my job, my particular skill, is sniffing out forgeries. Fakes, that sort of thing. And I'm really good at it. So good that I even have a nickname. They call me the 'Antiques Whisperer'. Which is a bit silly because I don't actually whisper to anything, and not all the things I don't whisper to are antiques – some of them are very modern – but it does convey the essential oddness of what I do.

Other experts in fakes are what you might call very scientific in their approach. They use science, in the form of chemicals, and X-rays, and tiny paint scrapings. They analyse the items scientifically and they're always sending things away to the laboratory (I don't know which laboratory or if there's a whole lot of different ones) for scientific tests. That's not what I do at all. Admittedly, I do do a bit of research, mostly reading because of the nature of the sort of items I'm called upon to investigate, but I haven't been in a laboratory since school and what I know about science wouldn't fill a shot glass. No, what I do is very different indeed.

What I do is I walk around the object. I look at it. I stare at it, quite hard. I might pick it up. I consult my notes, if I have any, and then I just think. All right, once I sniffed an object, and that did get mentioned by people. But it was a paperback book which was supposed to have belonged to Lawrence of Arabia and which had been found in a hotel reading room in Jedda, where he had apparently left it behind. Seventy years later an apparently casual visitor had opened it and seen Lawrence's name scrawled in it – but it smelled slightly damp. All that time, you see, in an arid climate in a dry room in the middle of a desert city and it was faintly damp. Even the sternest critic would have to agree that something was up with that. And indeed when the book was sent to the laboratory, for tests, they discovered that the tiny mould spores in the centre pages were native to Kircudbrightshire, a county that Lawrence of Arabia had never visited. As my dad used to say when he beat me at draughts, thus I win.

And that's what I do. I get an object with a disputed provenance – and I'm always the last resort, like those stupid psychics Scotland Yard get in when they're Baffled, not that I believe there's anything psychic about what I do – and I study it – always doing some reading around it, so I'm not completely whistling in the dark – and I see if I can get a *feel* for it, if there's some quality about it that's off, or not right. Sometimes I can't, and then I just have to throw in the towel and admit that I'm only human like the rest of them. But sometimes I get it right. And sometimes I don't just get it right, I get it spectacularly right. All boasting apart.

So here I am, driving along, listening to John Peel on a sunny morning, all because three weeks ago I got a call from Roger Armstrong at Pring's. Armstrong's one of those classic public schoolboys. You know the kind: slept in a dormitory for six years and got cold mash for dinner so he thinks he's served his time in the misery gulag and now he can drink brandy and tell people what to do for the rest of his life. I'm not bitter; I went to a public school myself, for a while, anyway, but there's a type, isn't there? And Armstrong is the type. Very useful in an auction house too, as you might imagine. Comes down in his old school tie, lovely voice, picks up a vase and says, 'My uncle had one of these. Beautiful piece.' Doesn't matter if his uncle had one or not or if he'd picked it up in Poundland, any client hearing that is going to go weak at the wallet.

I suppose Armstrong's my boss, although being freelance it's hard to say. Technically I could naff off somewhere else tomorrow, but Pring's pays me nicely to stick around so I do. And after the Lawrence of Arabia business, where my suspicions were not only proved right but also saved Pring's a shedload of money, they're very keen for me to stick around.

And so, one morning not very long ago, Armstrong called me.

'Bread,' he said, wasting no time or breath on manners or familiarity, 'can you come in this morning?'

'I've got a couple of things on, actually,' I said, even though I hadn't, because that's what you do. You're always busy even when you're not and you always take a day to do your work even when it actually only takes you an hour.

'This is important, Charles,' he said, with the tetchiness that comes from thinking that if you own half the country you therefore own half the people in it.

'Ooh,' I said, campily, because I know he hates anything like that, from Andy Warhol to *Are You Being Served?*, 'do tell.'

'I can't, not over the phone,' said Armstrong. 'Like I said, it's important.'

Having scraped off the veneer of charm to reveal the craquelure of unpleasant toff underneath, I felt my work was done.

'On my way,' I said.

Armstrong was waiting for me in reception.

'You all right, Roger?' I said. It's not always wise to wind up toffs – see King John for details – but he'd wound me up, so one–nil and thus I won.

He ignored me. He was looking at a large painting on the wall. It was of an imperious-looking young woman with a toy rabbit on her lap. It was both erotically charged (the woman) and creepy (the rabbit).

'I like it,' I said.

'You would,' said Armstrong. 'I think it's a piece of rubbish. Chocolate-box trash of the worst kind.'

'But it's Gus Honeybun,' I said.

'It's Robert Lenkiewicz, you ignoramus,' said Armstrong. He was in an excellent mood, I could tell.

'I know it's a Lenkiewicz,' I said. 'I'm from Devon, remember, and Lenkiewicz was a Plymouth artist. And that –' I pointed at the rabbit '– is Gus Honeybun. He was the rabbit who did the birthdays on TSW.'

'I have no idea what you're talking about,' said Armstrong.

'The woman is a television presenter called Judy Spiers,' I continued, but Armstrong had got bored of being wrong and was headed for the lift.

We got in. 'Judy Spiers did the birthdays with Gus,' I explained, more to annoy Armstrong than to enlighten him. 'Lenkiewicz must have been commissioned to paint them.'

'I don't care,' said Armstrong.

'He embalmed a homeless man and kept him in his front room,' I went on. 'Lenkiewicz, that is, not Gus Honeybun.'

Armstrong tried to quell me with a look. I decided he'd suffered enough and stopped talking. It doesn't do to wind up toffs too much.

The lift doors opened. 'This way,' said Armstrong and led the way into a small, very secure room. Inside the room was a table with a light inside it, the kind photographers use for looking at transparencies. On top of the table were a pair of cotton gloves and two pieces of paper. One piece was a sheet of A4 with printed writing and a signature, the other a photocopy of what looked like a page from a notebook.

Armstrong locked the door behind us.

'What's this then?' I said.

'You're the Antiques Whisperer,' he said with more than a touch of sarcasm. 'You tell me.'

I put on the gloves and picked up the first piece of paper. It was a letter, dated nineteen days earlier and, whatever it said, was clearly not the focus of Armstrong's urgency. I put it down again and picked up the photocopy. It was a copy of a piece of lined paper and was covered in a childish, slightly smudged pencil scrawl.

'I'm no expert in graphology,' I said, which I knew would infuriate him, especially if he'd actually got an expert in graphology to look at the page earlier. Judging by the date on the letter and the time elapsed since it was written, he almost certainly had. 'But this page was written by a child. Or someone trying to write like a child.'

'Is that it?' said Armstrong. 'I could have told you that.'

I ignored this.

'I need to see the actual letter,' I said. 'I can't get much off a photocopy. Do you have anything else to show me?'

Armstrong pushed the letter towards me.

Palmer House
East Budleigh
Devon
29.02.2017

Dear Mr Armstrong

I was given your name by Alan Curtis at Pring's office in Exeter as he said you were the man to speak to concerning modern items of interest (I understand that in this context 'modern' means anything less than one hundred years old).

I was clearing out an old chest of drawers in our home, which we have been sole occupants of as a family since 1977, and I came across a cache of old papers. Most were bills relating to the previous occupancy, but the contents of one notebook – from which I have photocopied an extract – reminded me of something. I am sure that from the infant handwriting and familiar prose you will recognise its origin as being an extract from, or even an early draft of, Miss Daisy Ashford's The Young Visiters.

In itself, I don't need to tell you, this is exciting news.
Even now, there are many fans of Miss Ashford's work
and The Young Visiters has been continually in print
since it was first published. But there is a more significant
element to this discovery.

Palmer House is not a famous house and has never been
home to the rich and famous. But it does boast one
'celebrity' claim – for a few days towards the end of the
First World War, JM Barrie was a house guest. (This fact
can be authenticated easily via photographs and local
newspaper accounts.) I am sure the significance of this will
not be lost on you.

I am therefore inviting you to peruse this tiny scrap of
paper, paying attention not just to the aforementioned
misspelt extract or draft, but also to its final, apparently
unrelated contents. I am sure that, once you have read and
digested those contents, you will wish to be in touch per-
sonally.

Yours sincerely,

Cora Vanstone

I handed the letter back to Armstrong. His face was more expectant
than an actual pregnant woman.
　'Well?' he said.
　'I don't get it,' I said. 'I know who JM Barrie is, he wrote *Peter Pan*.
But –'
　'Yes?'
　'Who's Daisy Ashford?'
　He sighed. 'I wonder about your education sometimes, Charles.'
　I don't wonder about yours, I thought, you Latin-stained anachro-
nism with your three years at Oxford and your four GCSEs. I smiled
pleasingly.

'Enlighten me,' I said.

'No,' he said. 'Look it up on the way.'

'On the way?'

'Yes. You've –' and he hesitated. 'You might be on to something with the handwriting business, that's all I'm saying. I can't commit to anything at this stage, but you need to get down there.'

I saw it then. The bit about not committing made it clear. There was money at stake, quite probably big money. This is a rule with dealers and auction houses: the bigger the stakes, the vaguer the statement. If the original notebook was somehow worth, say, a hundred quid, Armstrong would be fairly forthcoming about what he wanted; he might even actually tell me what he wanted. But if the paper was worth a lot of money, as it seemed to be, then Armstrong would be saying just what he was saying now, which was by and large nothing.

'You want me to go to Devon?' I said. 'With no information? No background and no plan?'

'That's right,' said Armstrong. 'Is that a problem?'

'No,' I said, 'It's what I do.'

I went back to my flat, put on my headphones to block out the neighbours – who had somehow contrived to have a massive argument about knocking through a supporting wall while at that exact moment actually knocking through a supporting wall – and consulted one of my many volumes of art history encyclopaedias. Did I hell. I went online and googled 'Daisy Ashford'.

The result wasn't what I was expecting. Pring's is what you might call a traditional auction house. They sell the kind of art that people look at and go, 'Oh look, art.' You know when someone says 'I don't know much about art but I know what I like'? Well, that's the kind of art that Pring's sells. Oil paintings. Watercolours. Statues. The odd icon. And first editions. Pring's are big on first editions, possibly because the first Pring had been friends with Andre Deutsch and Victor Gollancz and all manner of people who had publishing houses named after themselves because they were literally publishers, and not people who fronted multinational book companies which just happened to be named after people.

9

So Pring's were good on books, and manuscripts, and authors. And particularly children's authors. The original typed manuscript of *The Mouse and his Child*? Pring's sold that. A signed first edition of *The Phoenix and the Carpet*? Pring's had one. A copy of *The Magician's Nephew* inscribed by CS Lewis to JRR Tolkien? Pring's had two. Which was a bit of a problem, but Pring's solved it by getting experts in to examine each book independently. Somehow both books were verified real, and quietly sold to foreign collectors who, it was hoped, would never meet. Not totally kosher, but nothing was proved, or even intimated, and – who knows? – maybe Tolkien lost his copy of *The Magician's Nephew* and asked Lewis to sign another for him. It happens.

Anyway, even before googling Daisy Ashford, I could see why the letter's mentioning of JM Barrie would interest Pring's. JM Barrie is one of those rare writers whose life has almost overtaken his work. There are probably as many films, books and plays based on Barrie's life as there are based on his work (and his work, these days, is almost entirely forgotten by the general public with the massive and obvious exception of *Peter Pan*). But I couldn't see what Barrie had to do with this letter until I googled Daisy Ashford, and then it all became clear.

Sit back, pour yourself a large drink and get comfortable, because this is a story and a half.

At the time of the end of the First World War, JM Barrie was not just one of the best-known children's writers in the world, he was one of the best-known and most successful writers full stop. *Peter Pan* had run for nine years on stage and been adapted into a novel a few years later, ensuring Barrie's place in history and popular culture. Sometime late in 1918 or early in 1919, Barrie received an odd manuscript from Frank Swinnerton, an editor at the publishing house of Chatto and Windus. Swinnerton, himself a novelist, told Barrie that Chatto were publishing the enclosed manuscript and that it was 'a work of genius'.

Swinnerton's reason for approaching Barrie, apart from his fame, was clear. He wrote in his covering letter, 'We should really like very much to publish the work prefaced by some sort of assurance that it is the authentic work of a young person.' The manuscript enclosed appeared to offer little doubt that it was the work of a young person. It had been written in a child's exercise book and was full of spelling mistakes and juvenile grammatical errors.

It was called *The Young Visiters* and it had apparently been written by a nine-year–old girl called Daisy Ashford. A slim volume, to say the least, *The Young Visiters* was both charming and unintentionally hilarious as the author's prose veered in and out of the clichés of Victorian romantic fiction with unerring comic timing. The whole thing was, to Swinnerton's eye, delightful and he had no doubt that the book would be a hit. But it only worked as a book if it was clear that the writer was a nine-year-old girl. Hence his desire to involve Barrie, as some kind of authority on the voice of children.

Barrie not only confirmed that *The Young Visiters* was the work of a child (with some reservations about one or two lines which he felt had been 'meddled with') but, after a personal meeting with Swinnerton, agreed to write the preface. It was a wise decision. *The Young Visiters* was a publishing sensation. It was reprinted eighteen times in its first year. It has been dramatised, televised and filmed, and in 1920 spawned a hugely successful parody in the United States by the comic author Ring Lardner, entitled *The Young Immigrunts,* which details, in borderline–illiterate childish prose, a family journey through America.

Barrie's involvement, however, had one curious side effect, which was ironically the exact problem that Swinnerton had hoped Barrie's involvement would remove: many readers, noting just how perfect the world Miss Ashford had created was, suspected that a talented adult had in fact written *The Young Visiters.* An adult with both excellent writing skills and an ear for the rhythms of childish speech. You're ahead of me, I can tell. Basically, lots of people thought that JM Barrie wrote *The Young Visiters.*

And, judging by the carefully concealed excitement in her letter, one of those people was Cora Vanstone of Palmer House, East Budleigh, Devon.

'And in this meeting we had earlier on this evening, we were told that dif-

ferent DJs would be despatched to different urban centres to release various
balloons and so on and so on, you see. So goody goody, I cried, where am I
going? And they said, well, actually, Peelie, you're not going anywhere.'

John Peel's self-deprecating voice fills the car as I head towards the
Westway.

'I mean, everyone else is going. Even Gambaccini is going to somewhere
like Nottingham to fall over and release a great number of balloons invol-
untarily...'

Most radio DJs, historically, have always sounded like apes con-
sumed with excitement. Peel's voice was a much calmer proposition
and I found it soothing. This was going to be a long drive but I was
pretty much all prepped up and ready to go. I'd looked up Cora Vanstone and Palmer House on the net as well and not much had come
up. Palmer House wasn't on Zoopla, which meant it hadn't come up
for sale in decades, but its East Devon location and general taking-
up-spacery on Google Maps suggested it was worth a few bob. Cora
Vanstone had apparently owned a bijou art gallery in Budleigh Salterton and then sold it, but apart from that and the fact that Vanstone
was quite a common name locally, there was nothing.

JM Barrie's visit to Palmer House wasn't anywhere online, but there
was no real reason why it should be, unless he'd written Peter Pan
there or shot someone during his stay. So all I had to go on was the
letter, which was essentially devoid of useful content, and the notebook extract, which wasn't a lot of use to me because it was a photocopy. I don't want to be a ponce about this apparent skill of mine, but
for me to determine the provenance of something, I have to have the
actual object in my hands, not a copy of it.

So effectively I had nothing to go on. Fortunately, that's the way I
like it. You can keep your forensics and your carefully removed sam-
ples. All I want to do, in this case at least, is go down there, have a
look-see and draw my own conclusions. Not that this is always easy.
People in possession of the goods are generally suspicious of anyone
who wants to ask them a couple of questions and already I was imag-
ining Cora Vanstone to be a cut-glass pony-owning county lady with
tight white hair and matching cashmere sweater whose idea of coop-
erating would involve telling me my opinion and not letting me have

a proper look-see. There might even be a local solicitor around or, worse, a friend who knows a bit about antiques to further hinder me. Either way, my simple plan – look at document, form opinion about document – might not be that simple. I didn't really care about value; it's not my department and I don't even watch *Antiques Roadshow*, but even I could see that a manuscript which might be an early draft by Daisy Ashford is one thing, but a manuscript which might be by JM Barrie is, both historically and financially, another. So there would almost certainly be someone hovering, ready to offer useful financial advice, protect Cora Vanstone's interests and generally be, from my point of view, a complete pain.

But I could worry about that later. Right now I was just going to drive out of London in a big red Jag, listen to John Peel, and enjoy myself.

Or so I thought.

The Jag wasn't mine. I did own a car but it was horrible. It was a Ford something – I didn't know what because the thing with the name of the car on fell off years ago – and its only nod towards personality was that it somehow looked Romanian. Whenever people commented on it, they said, 'Is your car from Romania?' And I knew what they meant.

Anyway, my car was horrible, and as I was working in a field which values appearances, there was no way I was turning up at Palmer House in something faintly Romanian. Also I was on expenses. So I hired something suitable for the journey. Something that went with my tweed jacket (with leather elbow patches) and brown brogues. It's amazing how much these people judge you by the way you look and it's fascinating to see how you can change their opinion with clothing.

And cars. I went to see an old friend of mine, Ivor Wilson. Ivor ran a company that hired cars for TV shows and weddings, both of which value old vehicles and deception. He had a wide range of cars from every era – Capris and Minis, Rollers and Jensens – but I knew exactly what I wanted. It was a far-from-subtle bit of cultural referencing and about as subliminal as shouting I AM A TRUSTWOR-

THY ANTIQUES EXPERT in an old lady's face, but that was the point.

'Morning, Ivor,' I said, walking into his yard (I'd parked the Ford Something around the corner where I hoped it might get towed), 'I'm after something special.'

'Hi Charlie,' said Ivor, wiping his hands on a cloth I'm sure he kept solely to make customers think he was always tinkering with his cars (appearances, you see), 'What is it this time? Bentley? Bugatti?' He looked hopeful. 'Aston Martin? We've got a silver DB6 now.'

'I wish,' I said, wondering what a client might think if I turned up in a proper Bond car. They'd probably think I was on drugs. 'No, I was wondering if the Jag was in.'

'Which Jag?' said Ivor, although I could see by his nearly salivating face that he knew which one.

'The Morse Jag,' I said, and Ivor all but punched the air.

'The Mark 2? I'll have a look,' he said, and nearly knocked me over running to check.

Ten minutes later, I was shoving my way through West London traffic in a red Mark 2 Jag, the actual car that Inspector Morse drove. Well, not the actual one, but an identical one. Same interior, same exterior, same terrible fuel consumption... and with a real tape player.

Now, I know in this age of MP3s and streaming and whatnot that a tape player – that is, if the phrase is unfamiliar to you, a machine designed to play audio cassette tapes – is something of an anachronism. I say 'something of' but, given that vinyl records are socially acceptable again, and there is even genuine nostalgia for the atrocity that was the eight–track cartridge, the cassette tape seems to me to be the ultimate throwback to a vanished era. You are more likely to find a hipster with a working phonograph that plays 78rpm shellac recordings than someone who enjoys listening to cassettes. Even, dare I say, compact discs are less pariah-like than cassettes.

The Jag had, admittedly, been retrofitted with a cassette player but this did not bother me. It was a tape machine of the correct era and I could easily imagine Inspector Morse rummaging in the glove compartment for a Deutsche Grammophon cassette of whatever it was he listened to all the time. It was, also admittedly, the case that the car's original speakers had been replaced with a set that enabled me to play my Peel show cassettes at a volume which would have made the real–life Inspector Morse very angry indeed.

In decor, condition and style, the Jaguar was perfect for impressing the people I have to impress. It said that I valued beautiful things and specifically beautiful old things. It said that I knew quality when I saw it. It said that I also probably liked real ale and classical music and bound volumes of Victorian novels. And it said that I was absolutely trustworthy when it came to valuing your stuff.

It also said that I was someone who knew nothing about cars. The Jag did about six gallons to the mile, had a clutch like a sack of squid and, according to Ivor, was less reliable than his first wife, who had smoked crack at their wedding. I was taking a risk driving this gorgeous idiot of a car to Devon, but I was an AA member so they could fix it if anything went wrong – and indeed had on more than one occasion, the AA man wincing as he removed things from under the bonnet, like an archaeologist who feels the burial site should have remained undisturbed.

I also liked driving it because I'd read once that Morse drives a Jag only in the TV series. In the books, he drives a Lancia but the actor playing Morse wanted a British car. The idea of a work of fiction being fictionalised appealed to me no end.

The motorway beckoned. Nothing to do now but drive. And when you drive a Jaguar Mark 2, people do one of two things. They either slow down to gawp at your lovely old car, or they make a big thing of overtaking it, to show that they're not intimidated by it. On this occasion I was driving in the slow lane, which meant that my entire journey was filled with people either whizzing past me, honking and making gestures supposed to indicate that they were getaway drivers, or reducing their speed to a rubbernecker's crawl.

Normally, I just turned up the Peel and got on with it but this particular afternoon something wound me up. An oik in a cheap sports car wasn't just slowing down or speeding up. He was doing both. I first encountered him in my mirrors as he came out of a slip road and immediately started driving alongside me.

At the same time, he was apparently having an argument with his passenger, an attractive woman (they always are) who didn't seem to be enjoying this macho display. And then he raced off ahead to show that his dog on wheels was indeed the best car in the world, yes it is, who's the best car in the world, you are, yes.

Ten minutes and he was back, having got himself stuck behind a lorry. The same argument seemed to be going on, only now he was messing around with a mobile phone. I couldn't see his face, just a stupid tweed cap and a phone held in the air by the hand not holding the steering wheel, and then I realised that the oik was *trying to take a selfie*. With the Jag in the background. At seventy-five miles an hour.

This apparently done (with cars honking and overtaking in some panic around him and his lady passenger finally grabbing the phone from him), he overtook me again, slowed down to wait for me and overtook me again before vanishing up his own fast lane. The whole thing had left me, I now realised, a bit shaken up. I wasn't what you'd call an especially confident driver at the best of times and, behind the wheel of a bad-tempered and elderly car with surly manual gears, I was starting to lose it a bit.

A sign told me there were motorway services three miles ahead. It also said that tiredness kills and I should take a break. Three miles later, I did just that.

I like motorway service stations. They get a bad rap because people have vestigial memories of the old transport cafés of the '60s and '70s and the improved, but still horrific, services of the '80s where your choices were something horrible on a plate with chips or something horrible in a bun with fries. But now even the meanest services have a proper coffee shop, whilst the new posh services have Mexican take-away and noodle bars.

Mostly though I like the reassuring nature of motorway services. You go in and there's always a sprawling newsagents selling magazines and sandwiches but also camping stools and teddy bears dressed as naval officers. There's often a shop selling mobile phone accessories and it's usually opposite an amusement arcade which contains three fruit machines and, for some reason, a coin-operated massage chair. The toilets are fascinating too, enormous arrays of urinals with adverts for male incontinence products, always thronged with a thorough cross-section of male humanity: long-distance lorry drivers, half-cut fools on stag weekends, dads trying to get their kids to wee or poo, businessmen trying to make calls as they piss and at least one cleaner wondering when he'll see daylight again.

I read a news story once about a man who got stranded at a motorway services. His name was Ted Carroll and he was a rep for a fudge company (it's funny what sticks in the mind). Carroll's car was stolen while he was in the toilets at, I think, Gordano Services, and with it his wallet and all his cards and forms of ID. With nobody around to help him – amazingly, he'd even left his jacket with all his spare change in the car so couldn't even use a call box – Carroll suddenly found himself stranded at the services, a modern-day Robinson Crusoe.

But Ted was a rep and he had the gab. While he waited for his firm to find him or his wife to work out what had happened, Carroll used his gab to get free coffee, sandwiches and even, memorably, a change of clothes (he claimed later he'd just persuaded a holidaymaker to lend him a shirt, socks and underwear but the journalist interviewing Carroll noticed a white patch on his wrist where once a Tag Heuer had been). Full and comfortable, Carroll sat back and waited for help to come.

Unfortunately, what Ted Carroll didn't know was that there had been an extraordinary confluence of events while he was on the road. His firm – which consisted, essentially, of two people, one of whom was always on holiday – had ceased trading, almost instantly, after the sudden death of its active partner and the inability (or lack) of anyone concerned to find the holidaying one. At the same time, in a completely unconnected situation, Carroll's wife finally got up the courage to use his latest absence (which she suspected would involve a visit to a still-active old flame in Swindon) to move out of their home and start a new life.

Carroll, then, was both jobless and wifeless. With no family or close friends to wonder where he was (and the old flame always unsure if he was coming to Swindon or not), he was in a genuine and unknowing limbo. By the time he began to suspect something was wrong, it was late at night and he was very tired. A cleaner found him at 2am, sleeping in the cockpit of a jet-fighter game. Luckily for Carroll, the cleaner was a recent immigrant from Eastern Europe and inclined to be sympathetic.

And amazingly, this was Ted Carroll's new life for the next three weeks. Begging (though he called it 'blagging') during the day and sleeping wherever the cleaners weren't working at night. He washed and dried his clothes in sinks and showers when nobody was about, shaved when he'd blagged enough money to get a disposable razor from a vending machine, and lived on fast food and coffee. Towards the middle of the fourth week, however, he had become too noticeable, and the manager of the coffee shop had had enough of the genial but slightly alarming beggar bothering his customers. He called the police, who approached Carroll and offered, not unreasonably, to take him home. At which point, Carroll become alarmed and tearful, claiming that he was home and refused to go with them.

Ted Carroll had gone native, and it took a lot of persuading to get him to leave. But, I was told, he still visits Gordano Services, often for whole days, and even now has to be prevented from blagging shirts and coffees from passing holidaymakers.

I thought of Carroll as I walked back to the Jag. I have to admit, I wondered if this story could actually be true – for example, was he really able to beg clothing off people? – and decided that, inevitably, I would google his name as soon as I was at whichever pub or inn I'd be staying at that night. I pictured somewhere small, with a sloping floor and diamond-shaped glass in the windows, with a kettle and a slightly annoying shower.

I got back in the Jag and turned the key in the ignition – and the key snapped off. I stared at the half I was still holding for quite a few seconds, then jabbed at the section stuck in the ignition with the big half. I tried to pull it out with my fingers, but this didn't work. I swore to myself and thought for a minute. Then I got out of the car and went back inside the services.

'Excuse me,' I said to the young man in the newsagents. 'Do you sell tweezers?'

He looked at me for a few seconds, asked me to repeat the question, and then got a colleague to come over. The colleague, an older woman who presumably, like me, came from the ancient realm where 'tweezers' was a real word, listened to my question again and reached behind her, where there was an entire rack of tiny grooming products. She handed me a blister pack-sealed pair of tweezers. I paid for them and went back out to the car.

I sat in the front seat, opened the blister pack and tried to get a grip on the key. I tried again and again with no luck at all and I was about to go in for the fourth time when I suddenly realised that the back door of the car was open. Obviously I'd been unable to lock the Jag, and I didn't remember opening the back door... I leaned in and saw that my bag was missing. In it were my clothes, my washbag and – oh God, my laptop. I patted my pockets. I had my wallet still and my phone and, folded into an inside pocket, the letter and the scrap of paper from Cora Vanstone.

This was small consolation, though, and I spent several minutes walking around the car park swearing and balling my fists inside my pockets. I didn't want to give any casual observer, or indeed the actual thief, the impression that I had lost my cool, but the fact was I had not so much lost my cool as had my cool ripped from my hot living hands and kicked down the street.

I felt my face turning the same maroon shade of fury as the Jag, and willed myself to breathe deeply for a few minutes. My sole concession to boiling internal rage was that, instead of counting to twenty, I made a careful list – in alphabetical order – of all the insults I could think of.

Arseholes.

My first problem was who to call first, the police to report the theft of my laptop, or the AA to get the car fixed.

Bollocks.

I decided to call the police first, who seemed almost languid in their lack of concern and urgency.

Cockmunch.

I all but forced them to take down my details and then called the AA, who were helpful if slightly puzzled. They said they'd send someone within the hour and I was to go to a safe place and wait for their text.

After a thorough look under the car seats and in the boot, I went back inside the motorway services and bought a coffee. I looked in my wallet. I had one debit card and nine pounds in cash.

'Oh Lord,' I said to myself, 'Please don't let me be Ted Carroll.'

Armstrong called, which was strange. He very rarely called, partly because he didn't like me, and partly because he didn't have to.

'Hello, Roger,' I said, putting just the right degree of *why-are-you-calling-me?* into my voice.

'There you are,' he said, as if I'd been avoiding him. 'Listen, there's a problem.'

'What sort of a problem?'

'Cora Vanstone. I've left several messages but no reply.'

'On her mobile?'

'And her landline.'

'Have you tried emailing her?'

'She, doesn't seem to have email.'

'Oh, right.'

That's the trouble with working in the World of Antiquities. Too often you end up having to deal with people who like the past so much they wish they were living in it. People who say 'televisual receiver' when they mean 'telly', people who claim not to own DVD players, or even VCRs. People who actually cup their ears when you use crazy modern phrases like 'text' or 'mobile phone'. If I ruled the world, these people would be taken outside their thatched cottages and beaten to death with a rolled-up copy of the internet. But I don't rule the world and I have to be nice to them.

I decided not to ask Armstrong if he'd looked for Cora Vanstone on Snapchat and instead asked, 'Should I come back and wait for further instructions?'

'Might as well keep going,' he said. 'What we've done is we've sent her a postcard.'

'A postcard? Like you were going on holiday?'

'A plain postcard.'

'I see. So what do you want me to do?'

'Keep driving, obviously.'

'But what if she's not there?'

'Wait for her.'

'Outside her house?'

'If you want. That's not really for me to say.'

And he rang off. Lovely, I said to myself, and was about to enjoy a bout of swearing when my phone rang again. This time it was the AA, saying their man was on his way, but an emergency had come up and he'd be delayed. Then my phone beeped again. It was a different sort of beep, meaning that my battery was low and I should charge it. Not a problem.

I looked around the service station. There was a charging point nearby, but it cost a pound a session. Now I'm not a mean man, but the way I see it, electricity is just something that's lying around for the taking, and this place was full of it. So I took my charging cable and had a scout around until I found a plug socket in a nearby wall with a table and chair next to it. This way I could drink my coffee and check my emails on my phone while recharging for free. I saw there was a red label on the socket that said NOT FOR PUBLIC USE so, to avoid any finger-pointing, I put my coat at my feet so I could cover my phone. I plugged the cable into the phone and then, with some bending, managed to get the other end plugged into the socket. I flicked the socket switch to 'on'. There was a sudden fizz and a snap and I felt a small jolt of electricity. I dropped the phone, which was just as well as smoke was coming out of it and it smelled of melted plastic. I carefully unplugged it and looked at it. The charging cable was now fused to the body of the phone. Worse, the phone screen was blank.

How had this happened? I had no way of knowing, but I also had no intention of being blamed for this freak accident, so I moved to another table with my coffee. As I sat down, I realised that not only was I incommunicado, but that the AA man would have quite a job finding me. He had a description of the car, true, but it was a large car park and very full. I therefore had no choice but to head outside and keep an eye out for the thankfully very visible bright yellow AA van.

Two hours later, there was still no sign of the AA van and it was starting to rain. I've always thought that was an odd phrase – 'starting to rain' – because surely it's either raining or it isn't, rain doesn't have a bit of a warm-up before it rains, it just rains, but on this occasion 'starting to rain' was spot on, because first of all a small amount of rain came down, little drops here and there, and then there were uncomfortable, fat sploshy lumps of rain on my head, and then the rain just totally lost it and started really giving me what for. I put my coat on but it wasn't waterproof. I searched the Jag for an umbrella but there wasn't one. Then I had the bright idea of actually sitting in the Jag.

The rain hammered down on the Jag's roof and, far away, I could hear thunder. The effect was, curiously, rather soothing. I think for some British people – me, anyway – there's a powerful nostalgia invoked by sitting in an old car during a storm. Memories of seaside holidays, sitting in a car on a rain-blasted seafront, or at a campsite waiting until the sun comes out so you can put your tent up. I find it soothing, anyway, as I said. Which is probably why, leaning back on the fine upholstery, listening to the rain drumming on the car's exterior, I fell fast asleep.

I woke with a drool and a cricked neck and some alarm. It was evening outside and for a second I didn't just not know where I was, I didn't know who I was. I was in a dark space in the middle of nowhere and I couldn't remember my own name. I was breathing fast and my eyes were stretched wide open. I realised I was on the verge of a panic attack and began to breathe deeply, in and out.

I calmed down.

'You're in a motorway services car park,' I told myself out loud. 'You're sitting in a rented Jaguar and your name –'

I paused.

'Your name –'

This was ridiculous. I knew very well what my name was, but I just couldn't put my finger on it.

'Your name –'

I didn't want to do it. I really didn't. It felt like admitting defeat. I don't know who to or what kind of defeat, but it really did. I had no choice though. I reached into my jacket, took out my wallet and looked for a credit card.

'Your name – my name –'

I looked at the credit card.

'– is Charles Bread. Charlie Bread.'

I slumped back in the seat. The day was not going well. I decided to be positive. On the debit side, I'd lost my laptop, I'd fritzed my mobile phone and I'd fallen asleep and missed the AA (I imagined the driver looking around the car park, wondering why he'd not heard from me, and then deciding to go and assist someone who cared). But on the plus side, I had a wallet with fully functioning credit cards and there was a perfectly good hotel a few feet from where I was sitting.

I closed the Jag's door behind me, checked that I had all of my remaining possessions with me, and walked over to the service station hotel.

The room was – well, I liked it. It was small and new, like the rest of the hotel. The carpet was unstained, the sheets were white and crunchy, and there was a plethora of light, wood-effect furniture standing on bendy grey steel legs. Wi-Fi was available (albeit not to me) and there was a television and a kettle with sachets of coffee, sugar and milk substitute. After a few minutes wrangling the landline, I even managed to get through to the AA who were reasonably under-standing in the circumstances and agreed to send someone out in the morning. They couldn't give an exact time but they would phone my hotel room and let me know when they were on their way.

So the rest of the evening was, as they say, my own. I decided that I would have a shower and wander downstairs to the hotel's minia-ture restaurant which also, fortuitously, doubled as a bar, have some food and a drink, and then retire to bed, having first washed my shirt, socks and underwear in the sink and put them on a radiator to dry. The perfect end to a perfect day.

I was just about to set this plan in motion when I saw the newspaper. I don't really buy newspapers – I get most of my news online – and this was a tatty copy of some tabloid or other that I didn't even like. I wouldn't have given it a second glance if it hadn't been left open in the middle, and even then it might not have caught my attention were it not for a small photograph of a piece of sculpture.

A piece very well known to me.

Half an hour later, experiencing the mild physical unpleasantness that anyone feels when they've had a perfectly nice shower but then been compelled to put back on the clothes they've worn all day, I was sitting in the bar stroke restaurant with a small bowl of pasta and a large glass of red wine (capacity of bowl and glass: roughly equal) and trying not to think about what I'd read.

The picture was illustrating a report about a woman who'd been murdered. It told me a lot about the tabloid that they'd used a photo of the sculpture rather than the victim.

'The Rawley Vulcan,' said the caption, 'Centrepiece of the collection.'

The Vulcan was briefly mentioned in the piece, and the writer had clearly tried to connect the sculpture with the murder (the victim was the Rawley Collection's curator, Lily George, but there had been no theft, so it seemed coincidental, if awful). I put the newspaper to one side, ordered another whisky, and found myself drawn to unpleasant memories. Because the Rawley Vulcan, or rather the whole business that went with it, was the worst thing that I had ever been involved with.

CHAPTER TWO

'There are no standards. It's totally unregulated. You can shop around for a scientific report that probably says essentially what you want. It's shocking.'
— Nicholas Eastaugh, technical art historian

The Rawley Vulcan might not be as well known to the general public as it is to the art world or the antiquities community, but for a while it was big news. It is, as the name suggests, a small statue of the Roman god Vulcan, called Hephaestus by the Greeks, or the other way round, I'm not sure, and it's a lovely thing. Vulcan, as depicted, is a twisted little man, muscular and crippled at the same time, with a suitably demonic face that befits his role as the god of whatever it is, blacksmithing and furnaces and all that sort of thing. The Rawley Vulcan is in all the encyclopaedias as an example of seventeenth-century Italian sculpture at its finest, and the combination of red marble for the god's face and limbs with black jet for his robes and, entertainingly, eyebrows, is bold and dramatic and sets up a deliberate comparison with the more familiar figure of that other dweller in flames, Lucifer. There had initially been some doubt about the Vulcan's provenance. Brought back from Italy at the end of the First World War by the, I think, fourteenth Lord Rawley whose name was immediately attached to the sculpture, as though he'd made it himself and not just bought it, the Rawley Vulcan attracted comment not just for its beauty but for a few other things as well.

Firstly, there are very few statues, large or small, of Vulcan. As a god, Vulcan lacks the looks of Venus or Apollo and the drama of Jupiter or Mars. He's ugly, basically, and as most people in a position to have a statue made of something tend to go for something that's flattering to their person or at least representative of their alleged or desired character – like all those fat Georgians in wreaths dressed up as heroes of antiquity – it's very unlikely that someone would want to have a statue of the unattractive Blacksmith of the Gods. Therefore it's most likely that a sculptor would have made such a thing for himself, either as a private joke or because he identified with Vulcan in some way. And, while the maker of this statue neglected to write his name and address on the base of his work, as it turns out there was a sculptor who fitted the bill perfectly. His name was Aleijadinho.

Born Antônio Francisco Lisboa in the town of Ouro Preto, then called Vila Rica in what is now Brazil, in either 1730 or 1738, Aleijadinho was both talented and unfortunate. He created several memorable and valuable pieces whose beauty was, sadly, in direct contrast to his own looks. 'Aleijadinho' is the Portuguese for 'little cripple', and Lisboa acquired his new name when a mystery illness began to change his body into a possibly leprous new form. By the end of his life he was apparently sculpting with chisels tied to his hands. And it was this deformity which appears to be replicated in the Vulcan, whose hands are tight and clenched and whose tools are held unnaturally. That, and a passing similarity between the frowning, thunderous visage of the statue and Aleijadinho's own frowning, thunderous looks meant that the first scholar to properly examine the Rawley Vulcan made an imaginative leap and connected Aleijadinho to the statue.

After that it was an open–and–shut case. Several other pieces by Aleijadinho were clearly similar in important ways. The use of marble was identical. Aspects of the moulding, apparently, were definitively linked to certain furnaces in eighteenth–century Portuguese colonies. And so on. Provenance duly established – or established well enough to satisfy the critics of the day – the Rawley Vulcan settled down to enjoy a century and a half of being admired by visitors to Rawley House, being photographed for art history books (and county magazines) and eventually coming to the attention of Pring's, which was where I first became aware of it.

Armstrong had sent me some photographs of one of two items that he told me the Rawley Collection was thinking of selling on. They were an odd mixture, to say the least: some inferior portraits from the early twentieth century, a few atlases of dubious provenance and so on. The Vulcan was head and shoulders above the rest in quality. I sat down and opened the folder of pictures Armstrong had sent to me.

Ten seconds later, I was on the phone to him.

'Roger? It's Charlie. Charlie Bread.'

'It's half past nine.'

'I know. Listen, I'm looking at the photos you sent me from the Rawley.'

'Very conscientious. I'm watching *Fast & Furious* 7. What do you want, Charles?'

'Roger, I need to see the Vulcan. At once.'

There was what you might call silence at the other end of the line, if by silence you meant 'loud, annoyed breathing'. And then Armstrong said, 'Jesus, really?'

'Yes.'

'All *right*,' he said and put the phone down.

The next morning I was in a taxi to Rawley House. I whiled away the journey reading a *Daily Mirror* someone had left on the back seat. We arrived fairly promptly and, as I got out of the cab with the paper still in my hand, Armstrong was there to meet me. This was unusual but I soon saw the reason: a few yards away in the doorway was the Rawley Collection's curator, a tight-lipped woman in her late thirties called Lily George. (In the light of recent events, I wished now that I could have thought less ill of her. But it was too late now.)

'Watch out for her,' said Armstrong as we walked towards Lily, who was standing by a tiny desk looking pre-vexed, 'She's snippy at the best of times.'

And indeed Lily had the look of someone who was permanently on the verge of telling you that if you break it, you have to pay for it. Well, she wasn't going to like what I had to say, but she could lump it, I thought.

'We need to see the Vulcan,' said Armstrong (I could have said it just as easily but I didn't go to Marlborough so Lily wouldn't have been able to hear me. I don't have a chip about that sort of thing – it's just the way of the world – but it's tiring not being posh in the art world).

'Why?' said Lily.

To his credit, Armstrong didn't say, 'What's it to you? You're the caretaker. Now sod off and get it for us.' He said, 'This is Mister

Bread. He works with us in a freelance capacity. He'd like to see the Vulcan before it goes up to London for the sale.'

Lily made a face that would have got a teenager slapped in the old days, and turned on her heel. Armstrong raised an eyebrow at me as we went after her down a corridor covered in paintings of people whose disapproval seemed to follow us down the hall.

A few minutes later, we were standing in front of a display case in an anteroom. Although the Vulcan was supposed to have been packed for transport to London, clearly this moment was being delayed as long as possible so that the Rawley Collection could get as much gawper revenue as possible from the statue. And it was a beautiful thing. The face was mischievous and demonic, but also hinted at an inner pain. The body was likewise twisted while suggestive of physical grace. And there was childish delight to be had in the intricate detailing of the tools of Vulcan's trade – his hammer, his anvil, his apron...

'Can you remove it from the case, please?' I said to Lily George. She ignored me with the ease of long practice and said to Armstrong, 'This is highly irregular.'

Sometimes I think you can divide the world into two kinds of people, those who would never even conceive of using expressions like 'This is highly irregular' and those who never say anything else.

'Are you all right, Charles?' said Armstrong, and I realised I looked a bit tense. In fact, I was feeling extremely tense. I wasn't looking forward to finding what I believed I was going to find.

'May I?' I said and, without waiting for a tut from Lily, gently picked up the Vulcan. It hardly weighed anything and somehow its lightness seemed to be part of its beauty. I made a big show of examining it, even turning it over (gasp of horror from Lily George) to look at the base. Then I put the Vulcan gently back on the velvet cloth. And, again without asking permission, I took a photo of it with my phone. For the look of the thing, I turned the statue round and took a picture of the back, but I didn't really need to. Then, as if as an afterthought, I picked it up again and photographed the base.

'Thank you,' I said to Lily, in lieu of setting fire to all the paintings in the room, and I turned to Armstrong. 'Might I have a word, Roger?'

And before Lily George could allude once more to the irregularity of the occasion, high or otherwise, we were out of there.

I steered Armstrong into the corridor. He glared at me.

'All right, *Bread*. We've done your antiques detective bit and probably really pissed off our client. What's this about?'

I didn't say anything. I was sad, but I was also enjoying this.

'Look at this,' I said. I showed Armstrong the photo I'd taken of the front of the Vulcan.

'Yes, I've seen it,' he said. 'About three minutes ago.'

'Look at the apron,' I said. 'Look at the coat of arms.'

'What about it?' he said.

And then I showed him the back page of my *Daily Mirror*.

'Oh, crap,' he said.

We went to a café. Armstrong looked again at the photograph of the coat of arms, the two mallets *en saltire*, which is the heraldic term for 'crossed', and, on the back page of the *Daily Mirror*, a report on a recent West Ham game, which featured West Ham's logo of two crossed hammers as illustration. Or, if you're a herald, two mallets *en saltire*.

'It's a coincidence,' he said.

'It's a forger's joke,' I said.

'Shut up!' Armstrong all but hissed at me. Clearly 'forger' was not a word to be said anywhere.

I pressed on. 'Vulcan's a smith, right? He makes stuff out of iron.'

'He's not a footballer, though, is he?' said Armstrong. 'He doesn't play for Roman Gods United at the weekend.'

'West Ham used to be called Thames Ironworks, 120 years ago,' I said. 'That's why their coat of arms is a pair of hammers. Whoever made this threw in a little visual gag for their own enjoyment.'

'But it's eighteenth century,' said Armstrong. 'It's older than West bloody Ham.'

'If we had this dated...'

'We're not having it bloody dated!'

'But if we did, I think we'd find it was very much not eigh-teenth century. I think we'd find it was a beautifully made late nine-teenth or early twentieth-century pastiche.'

Armstrong sat back.

'I don't get it,' he said. 'Why would someone go to all this trouble?'

'To make the fake? Money,' I said. 'To put in the clues? Vanity. Ego. The main thing that trips up forgers is the urge to confess. Look at Van Meegeren. Couldn't wait to spill the beans. Lothar Malskat? Falling over himself to show the world how clever he was. Nope, someone commissioned this – yeah, about a hundred years ago – to fool Rawley or whoever, and someone else signed it with a couple of jokes.'

Armstrong looked at me. 'Clues, plural,' he said, 'Jokes, plural. You mean there's more than the coat of arms?'

I showed him the third photo, the base of the piece that historians have often felt might be a later addition from the use of certain pig-ments in the porcelain. In minute letters was a Latin motto.

'*Mallei in perpetuum*,' I said. 'Which is Latin for...'

'I know what it's Latin for,' said former public schoolboy Roger Armstrong. 'It's Latin for "Hammers Forever".'

Armstrong gave me a lift back to London, not so much out of human kindness as a desire to ensure that we didn't run into Lily George again. As we drove, Armstrong swore constantly and uninventively under his breath. Finally, once we had entered London and were coming up to Shepherd's Bush Green, he seemed to come to a deci-sion about something and pulled over in the forecourt of a garage.

'You're OK for petrol,' I said, mostly just to break the uncompan-ionable silence.

'We need a plan,' said Armstrong.

'I suppose we tell Lily to take the Vulcan out of the sale –' I began.

'No,' said Armstrong. 'We don't.'

'But it's a fake.'

'It's a fake in your opinion,' Armstrong said. 'According to all the experts – the real experts – it's completely genuine.'

'A series of thorough tests would establish that it's not.'

'There isn't going to be a series of thorough tests.'

'Why not? We can't go round flogging stuff that's not right.'

Armstrong turned to me. His face was quite red.

'Listen, you arsehole. We're not a charitable foundation. We're not a museum. We're an auction house. We sell stuff. And that's it. You think the Vulcan is the first... item of questionable provenance that Pring's has shifted? Really? In seventy years you think this is the only time something not quite a hundred per cent pukka has passed through our hands?'

'No, but –'

'No but nothing. We start telling people that our stuff isn't pukka and they'll think we don't know our business. They won't trust us any more.'

'This isn't about trust...'

Armstrong undid his seatbelt so suddenly that I thought he was going to lean over and strangle me.

'This is all about trust, Bread. Trust is all we have. People come to us with their vases and their pictures and their thing they had in the attic because they trust us. And if we start pissing about with their trust... well, other auction houses are available.'

I was feeling stubborn, I guess.

'We're not crooks, though, are we?'

'No, we're not. Most of what we do is above board and we do keep an eye out for dodgy gear. But we don't do product recall. We don't put an ad in the paper saying, if you have purchased a shonky Mona Lisa from us, pop by and we'll give you a refund.'

He could see that I still wasn't entirely convinced.

'Let me put it this way,' Armstrong said. 'You know Andy Warhol?'

'I know of him, yes.'

'About ten years ago, the Warhol Foundation – the official heirs and legal maintainers of Andy Warhol's work – were asked by a collector to authenticate a Warhol self-portrait that he'd bought. Fairly reasonable request, you'd think, and also fairly reasonable that, since he'd asked them to do it, he'd abide by their decision.'

'I suppose so.'

'Well, he didn't. They told him his Warhol was a fake and he sued them. He sued the Andy Warhol Foundation, the presumable world experts on what is or isn't a Warhol, for doing something that he had asked them to do.'

'Yes, but surely he didn't win?'

'No, he didn't win, Bread. But it cost the Foundation seven million dollars in court to defend itself. And now they don't authenticate Warhols any more. Get out of the car.'

'Pardon?'

'You can walk from here. Have a think about the mess you nearly caused. The shedload of crap you could have brought down on our heads.'

I undid my seatbelt and got out of the car. He wound down his window and said, 'This isn't some nice quiet library where we all sit around discussing the history of antiquities, Bread. This is the Wild West.'

I waited until he'd gone round the corner and hailed a cab home. As we trundled towards central London, I wondered what I was going to do. And after a while, I realised I wasn't going to do anything. I could go to the Rawley Collection and tell them their Vulcan was a fake but I was fairly sure their attitude would be the same as Armstrong's: keep quiet and sell it on. They had more incentive to do so, after all, presumably having been bilked a century ago. I could warn whoever bought the item, but that might again create the same reaction, or worse. In either scenario, someone would certainly end up taking legal action against Pring's, which would pretty much ensure that I'd never work again, anywhere. The same would apply if I went straight to the law, which for some reason was the option that least appealed to me. Perhaps because, as an instinctive 'expert' rather than a trained one, I would be subjected to mockery by counsel. I could hear an imaginary QC in my head now: 'And you just "picked it up and had a look at it", did you, Mister Bread?'

No: there was, I realised glumly, no alternative. I was just going to have to keep my mouth shut. Pring's would be reassured that I was onside and unlikely to blab (I was slipping into Armstrong's public school slang, I realised) and they would regard me as a valuable insider, still extremely useful for spotting fakes – sorry, 'irregularities' – before Pring's had committed to selling them. (Which was, of course, exactly why I was called in by Armstrong to investigate the alleged JM Barrie documents.)

From now on, I was a colluder, if that's a word. I was a collaborator, someone who worked for Pring's interests and nobody else's. It was a shameful moment, and I knew I'd never feel the thrill of discovery or unveiling in the same way again. But I still had a job, I still had a reputation, and I would still be allowed to be the Antiques Whisperer.

And now Lily George was dead. The article said that she'd been shot, and her body had been found by a cleaning woman. There was nothing else, bar a few lines explaining how valuable the Vulcan was. It was a sad obituary for a career, to become a footnote in your own epitaph, upstaged by a sculpture.

I drank a silent toast to Lily George's memory – I owed her that at least – and was about to engage in man's ancient struggle to discover if I was supposed to pay my bill at the bar or summon a long-vanished waiter when I heard a commotion just outside. A couple, a man and a woman I thought, but it was hard to see in the dark. And then the woman came in. She was extremely striking, tall with long blonde hair and an angry expression that was probably related to the conversation she'd just had.

I would have noted this, stood up and gone looking for someone who would let me pay my bill had it not been for two things: firstly, I was overwhelmed by the bafflement and resignation you feel when you see someone who is very attractive in the company of someone you would pay to have assassinated, and secondly, I recognised her. She was the girl in the sports car with the oik.

This was, naturally, slightly puzzling. I'd been here for several hours, and I was the one driving slowly. Even if the oik and the girl had stopped off in a nearby hamlet to annoy some locals, he should still have been here some time ago. I couldn't think of anything that might detain an oik with a sports car for so long. Then it came to me. The oik had clearly been hoping to have dinner at the motorway hotel with the girl and then spend the night here, because they were having an affair. Perhaps there were other explanations but this was the most obvious. And it was a good plan: why risk being spotted in the town where you live when you can meet up in the most transient place imaginable, a kind of town which has no locals because nobody really lives here. My god, I thought, the whole place is probably packed to the rafters with adulterers. It must be the clandestine bunk-up capital of Southern England. I looked around and suddenly all I could see were couples, huddled over their drinks and wondering who would be the first to suggest going upstairs for a cramped shag.

I sneaked another glance at Oiky's girlfriend, who was studying a dog-eared menu like she was about to be tested on it, when a waiter appeared from nowhere with a card machine and I paid my bill. When I looked up again, the woman was engaged in a heated, if muted, conversation on her mobile. Then she looked at her phone, shoved it back in her bag and looked around for a waiter, clearly ready to delete the last few minutes from her mind and enjoy a drink. As she looked around, our eyes briefly met. She flashed an angry look at me and turned away again. I pretended to look at my credit card receipt. And then I did something that, as it turned out, would have a major effect on – I do not exaggerate here – the rest of my life. I put my hand up and summoned the waitress over to order another drink.

And so we sat there, the woman and I, at our respective tables, drinking our separate drinks and avoiding looking at one another as the evening went on and the bar stroke restaurant filled, then emptied, and then began slowly to ease into the night.

I was on my fourth whisky, I suppose, when a voice next to me said, 'Are you going to sit there all night?'

I looked up, and there was the woman. She was holding her glass of wine and giving me a look which I found hard to interpret. There was a bit of amusement in there, but not a patronising 'look at me being amused by you' amusement. There was a slight hint of annoyance and – I could have been wrong, but I am quite good at reading expressions – a bit of sadness too. Either way, she had come over to talk to me and she wasn't actually shouting or crying, so I had nothing to complain about.

I didn't say anything, just got up and pulled a chair out for her to sit on, which she did.

'I've been watching you,' she said. 'Watching you watching me. You have a quick glance and then turn away as soon as I look back at you. Or you look at my reflection in the window like you don't know I can see your reflection too. It's very annoying. If you want to talk to me, just talk to me.'

'I'm sorry,' I said. 'It's a habit. People–watching.'

'You weren't people-watching anyone else,' she said. 'You weren't sneaking looks at that old man over there. Or looking down his top.'

'I wasn't looking down his –' I stopped. She was grinning.

God, I like people who grin. I think I can forgive anything of anyone who grins. Big smiles that say, 'Ah, what the hell, everything's a laugh, eh?' I may be exaggerating, but people who grin are rarely pillocks. I bet Hitler never grinned. Stalin. The Reverend Jim Jones. Morrissey. Not a grinner among them. But this woman, this blonde woman in her expensive dress, holding her glass of wine like she might forget it if she let it go, she was a grinner.

'Got you,' she said.

'All right,' I said. 'I'll tell you the truth.'

And I did. More or less. Leaving out the bit about continuing to stare at her because she was also very attractive and I'd had four whiskies. I told her about the motorway and the oik in the sports car (I didn't call him the oik) and wondering what they were doing together (I didn't bring up the idea of an affair).

'Greg,' she said when I'd finished explaining. 'What a tosser. I'm sorry about him.'

'He's not your fault,' I said. 'I mean, it's not your fault.'

'He's got this thing about Jags,' she said. 'Passive–aggressive macho crap. Like he keeps saying he hates them, and he'd rather have his whatever his stupid hairdresser car is called, and then whenever he sees a Jag, he chases after it like a dog after a string of sausages.'

'A string of sausages?' I said.

'A string of sausages,' she said, and tried to look serious. Then she gave up, and snorted instead.

'My name's Penelope,' she said.

'Charles,' I said, then corrected myself. 'Charlie.'

'Nice to meet you, Charlie,' said Penelope. 'Shall we go to the pub?'

I looked at her.

'There's a pub?' I said. 'At a motorway services?'

'No,' she said. 'In the village.'

I looked blank.

'The village where I *live*.' She gave me another amused look. 'You don't think I'm staying in this hotel, do you?'

Walking in the dark has never been my greatest skill. And it is properly dark in the country. It hadn't been so bad when we'd escaped the confines of the services, crossing some grassy hinterland which was still lit up by the lights of the motorway, but as Penelope led us further away from the services and into some actual real countryside, the narrow lanes with their looming hedgerows and overarching trees seemed to fold in on themselves and I found myself starting to feel a bit claustrophobic.

'Are you all right?' said Penelope, who was wearing a large coat and, I now noticed, fairly sensible footwear.

'I'm fine,' I said. 'It's just very... dark.'

'No it's not,' she said. 'Look up, there's a quarter moon.'

'I can't look up,' I said.

She stopped. 'Why not?'

I hesitated. 'Because I'm scared of the stars.'

Instantly I wondered why I'd said that. I mean, it was true, but I wouldn't tell anyone that in a million years. Except I just had. I expected Penelope to laugh now, but she didn't. She just said 'I'm sorry. It's not far now' and walked on ahead, a bit more slowly than before.

The pub was everything a pub should be. It had a stone fireplace with a lot of ironmongery in it, some very old men who were talking to each other in either rural dialect or Aramaic, a dog that smelled of all the dogs in the world and a landlord who, despite it being impossible, gave every indication in his appearance and manner that he had flown Spitfires in the Second World War. Only the presence of a battered CD jukebox and a couple of vaping bikers suggested that this pub hadn't been built by some kind of olden–days public house reconstruction society.

'Nice pub,' I said to Penelope as I set our drinks (we were, perhaps unwisely, on the bitter now) down on an actual beaten-copper round table.

'I think so,' she said. 'So tell me, why are you frightened of stars?'

I like people who grin, but I'm not so keen on people who like suddenly asking direct questions. Still, she had at least waited until we were inside in the warm and the light to ask, so I said, 'Please don't mock me, but... when I'm out at night and there's no clouds, I just become completely aware that we're... we're on top of a great ball spinning in space and what's above us could equally be said to be below us. And I see myself upside down, with my feet sticking to the ground somehow, and below me is this enormous bowl of just the stars, lighting up darkness and nothing.'

It was a long speech, so I ended it by drinking most of my beer. Penelope looked at me with concern in her eyes.

'Before we leave,' she said, 'I'll order you a cab so you don't have to walk back.'

After that, the rest of the evening was fairly normal. We told each other what we did, which mainly meant I told Penelope what I did and she expressed amazement that someone could earn a living doing that. She was vague about her own means of employment, and everything else really. The beer was kicking in as well at this point, but I do remember going on about the Jag and the broken key in a kind of obsessive verbal loop, and her telling me a funny story about Greg, the oik, and how he'd had some sort of cosmetic surgery procedure on his chin to make it bigger.

And then I think the cab came, and there was some business with trying to get our coats on, and some friendly cheering as I made it out of the door, and the next thing I remember was waking up on a hotel bed with a beermat on my forehead.

Then there was something beeping by the bed, someone knocking on the door and the TV was on, so my head – which would have quite happily spent the day empty like an abandoned lighthouse – was not happy. The beeping was the phone, presumably asking me to check out, and the knocking was a cleaner, and the TV was showing a property show, which at least instilled in me the desire to get out. So I got up, stuffed my dirty clothes into a plastic laundry bag and spent some time under the shower, fighting a billowing and greasy shower curtain whose sole desire seemed to be to enter me from behind.

I decided not to shave as nobody was going to see me today and besides my skin hated me. After a moment's slow and awful thought, I took my clothes from yesterday out of the laundry bag and put them back on again. I saw the beermat lying on the rumpled bed and was about to put it in the bin when I saw writing on it. PENELOPE, it said, and a blurred email address. I put it in my pocket and headed downstairs.

I knew my clothes were lacking a certain freshness when the girl behind reception told me to put my key in the express checkout slot before I'd even reached the counter. I was about to check my pockets for my phone when I remembered it was dead. I approached the girl to see if I could use the hotel phone – I wished I'd remembered the phone in the room now – but she held up a hand to keep me away from the counter and said, 'There are a couple of messages for you, sir' and all but threw an envelope towards me.

I made myself complicit in her game of stink, gingerly lifted the envelope from the counter and went outside. I found my car, sat inside with the windows rolled down and opened the envelope. It was, to my great surprise, a message from Ivor. He had received a call from me, apparently, at 10pm the night before and would be with me – at my apparent suggestion – at 11.30 or so in the morning. I had no memory of making this call, which wasn't surprising, but it did seem like a sensible thing to have done, or, as it were, to have not done.

It was 11.15. I went back into the service station, discovered a shop called Natural Fibres Inc. and bought some socks, shirts and under-pants, all made from the least-natural fibres possible. I undressed in a toilet cubicle, feeling like a sordid superhero, put on my air-loathing new clothes and returned to the car park, where Ivor was just parking next to the Jag. An everyday occurrence, perhaps, but to me it felt like the sunrise on a new era.

Ivor wasn't best pleased. Jag keys are not easy to come by and he had a devil of a time getting the broken one out. He was also unimpressed that I hadn't stayed by my vehicle all night, while my unshaven face suggested to him that I'd messed up his car through drunkenness. But then, just as I had decided he was going to take the car off me, he smiled.

'She sounded nice, though,' he said.

'Who did?' I said.

'The girl,' said Ivor. 'Penelope. She was very funny, said you were too pissed to call me but you kept going on and on about the Jag. So she went through your wallet, found my card and rang me.'

Mystery explained, I thought, and watched as Ivor carefully and deliberately explained how to put a car key in the ignition without snapping it off.

'OK,' he said, getting back into his own car, 'Don't break this key, will you? And call me before you return the car. I don't want any hor-rific surprises, like the wheels have come off or you've converted her into a stock car.'

I waved ironically at Ivor as he drove off, and remembered that my mobile phone was dead. Something else to sort out, I thought, as I loaded my bag of travel-used clothes into the boot and headed back onto the motorway.

The record is stuck on its intro, the vocal repeating until Peel takes it off.

'That was almost Paul Collins, from the LP An Anthology of New Music, *anyway. Just imagine it, if you like. I'll give you a few seconds...'*

On 28 June 1979, John Peel is in a good mood, chatting about the failure of the song to play before segueing into a Sugar Minott track. Nearly forty years later, I too am in a good mood, because this is one of my favourite tapes. I hadn't planned to become a mobile archive of a DJ and national treasure when I started downloading old John Peel shows and transferring them to tape a year or two back, but once I began I found the process quite addictive. Which is why, even though I did have a clear idea what I was looking for, I didn't mind the odd diversion away from my main mission.

Also Peel was a fascinating figure, someone I could identify with. Like me, he'd been at a minor public school, destined presumably for some Dickensian mid-level future, perhaps a solicitor's office, maybe the civil service. And like me, he'd escaped that fate when, thanks to his love of music and his move to the USA just as the Beatles became famous, he found himself working as a radio DJ in Texas. Returning to the UK in the mid '60s, he served as a pirate DJ for a while and then joined Radio 1, where he was, essentially, the voice of whatever the current alternative to mainstream rock and pop was from 1967 to his untimely death in 2004.

While I'm currently having something of a punk and new wave jag – this era being, as it were, one of the most creative of Peel's career – I like to randomly delve back into Peel's other eras. The beat years of *Top Gear* (not that one). The hippy dippy *Perfumed Garden* (live sessions from poets with bongos). The twee indie pop of his '80s and '90s shows. The happy hardcore and grime of Peel in the early twenty-first century. Each era has one thing in common: a clear break between the last type of music Peel favoured, and an equal break with his previous audience, who would invariably declare that Peel had 'lost it' or was 'trying to sound cool' to a younger audience. Meanwhile John Peel, stately as a galleon, sailed on oblivious.

'It's all a bit rough on us Babylonians though, innit really? That was Sugar Minott and Captain Sinbad, with Hard Times Pressure...'

The Jag handled well. It was a pleasant car to drive, even if it was hungry for petrol and on a warm day the interior started to smell like the 1960s. But it covered the miles effectively and soon I found myself, unsurprisingly, on the outskirts of Reading. I say 'unsurprisingly' because anyone who drives west from London soon finds that a disproportionate part of their journey seems to take place on the outskirts of Reading. Reading I'm sure is a big place, but not so big that, wherever you are on the motorway or the A roads, you are almost always on the outskirts of Reading. It's as if Reading follows you around the country, like a huge, low cloud of buildings and retail parks, never quite in front of you or on top of you, but just close enough for you to be perpetually on its outskirts. Or so I thought as the Peel show ended and I looked at the Jag's elegant dashboard clock and realised that it was pretty much lunchtime. And I'd had nothing to eat since the pasta from the night before.

I was hungry, and there was nothing for it. I was going to have to go to a Three For One Inn.

There used to be a lot of Three For One Inns. There's not as many of them as there used to be, and you only really come across them in south-east England, but they're still around, and I love them. They're so – this is an oxymoron I know but it's right – so brilliantly fake. Everything about them is designed to allude to some imaginary aspect of the past, and every single allusion collapses on its arse, but it just works. Just as Frankenstein's monster is more than a jumble of other people's limbs and organs, Three For One Inns are much more than the sum of their parts.

This Three For One Inn was no different. Its exterior was both lean and mock Tudor, suggesting that it had begun its career as a roadhouse, one of those 1930s drinking and eating establishments for motorists on their way to a dirty weekend in Weston-super–Mare. There was a sort of mill wheel in the garden, put there for no other reason than there was room in the garden to put a mill wheel. The garden itself contained a modern play area and some benches with little purpose–built flowerpot–shaped ashtrays, to make smokers feel a bit more rural. (You could if you were bored, or mad, write a fascinating essay about the evolution of the flowerpot ashtray, from its roots as an actual flowerpot to its current status as a vaguely flowerpot–like item with grooves in the side. But I wouldn't if I were you.)

Inside, the magic really began. The decor was a mixture of traditional (mirrors, wooden chairs and tables, a huge stone fireplace) and modern (a shiny plastic counter, huge TV screens and a wall of arcade games both old and new). The menus managed to be both enormous – pages and pages covered with photographs of huge dinners – and limited, as close inspection of the text revealed they only did about six different meals, most of which involved chips. There was an excessive interest in dessert, with Rocky Roads, Key Lime Pies and Sticky Toffee Puddings suggesting that some people came here to die, not to eat.

And everywhere there were signs advertising and explaining the Inn's unusual name. If there were three of you, you could get – on some meals – three meals for the price of one. This explained the fact that at almost every table there were trios of diners, some obese, some not, some young, some old, but all cramming their gobs with sixty-six per cent–off food.

None of which applied to me, of course. I was on my own. I took a menu and went up to the bar.

'I'd like a cod and chips, please,' I said, 'and a pint of Coke.'

'Anything else?' he said.

'No, that's fine.'

'If you order two more meals, we'll reduce your bill down to one meal.'

'I'm only ordering one meal.'

'Are you sure? Perhaps if you were to ask those two gentlemen to join you, they could make up a meal–deal trio.'

And he nodded in the direction of two men at a table by the window. This was a bit odd. I had never heard of a Three For One Inn whose policy was to invite strangers to join one another to save money.

The men, too, were a bit odd. One was quite tall, with the bearing of an old-fashioned civil servant, and would have looked perfectly normal sporting a bowler hat and an umbrella. The other was smaller and round like a ball with arms. They could almost have been conceptual artists, or a retired stand-up duo.

Either way, I didn't like the look of them much and I had no intention of joining them for anything, especially a meal.

'No thank you,' I said, more prissily than I'd intended to, 'I'm dining on my own.'

'If you're sure,' he said.

'I'm sure,' I said. I had no intention of making up a lunchy threesome with anyone, let alone a pair of complete strangers. But to my horror, one of the men was approaching us now.

'I did ask him,' said the barman. I stared at him. Clearly I was part of some bizarre meal–deal honey trap.

'And he said no?' said the man, in a slightly European accent.

'I said no,' I confirmed. 'I'm really just here for a quick meal and off again.'

'But it would represent a substantial saving,' said the other man.

Now his companion was coming over. This was getting a bit weird.

'He said no,' said the first man to his companion.

'Did you tell him it would represent a substantial saving?' said the other man.

'Yes,' said the first man. 'He doesn't seem to care.'

'Look, I'm sorry,' I said, although I wasn't. 'I don't want to share my lunch with you. I don't even know you.'

The pair of them and the barman just gazed at me.

'I know,' I said desperately. 'How about we order together but I eat on my own at my table and you two gents eat together at your table?'

'Oh no,' said the barman. 'That's not how a Three For One Inn works.'

'We would have to eat together or not at all,' explained the first man.

'Then not at all it is then,' I said and walked out.

As I left I heard the first man call to me but I didn't register what he said until I was outside in the car park again. He said, 'Sooner or later, you will make a deal with us.' Which made no sense at all.

I was fuming as I got into the Jag. Worse, I was very hungry. I needed to do something to cheer myself up right away. Then I remembered the beermat that Penelope had left on my forehead last night.

I took it out of my pocket and once again tried to decipher her bitter-blurred handwriting. The first word – Penelope – was easy enough to read. Then there was an @, and something that could be 'earwig' or 'easy' or 'eager', and then something that was probably '.net'. I took my laptop out of my bag, logged into Wi-Fi and typed in penelope@easy.net. I also had a go at penelope@eager.net and then, somewhat optimistically, penelope@earwig.net.

Hello, I wrote, *I hope this is the right Penelope. I'm the man who you helped with his Jaguar problem. You can find me at this email address. Best wishes. Charlie Bread.*

I pressed Send and drank my coffee. I had low expectations, to say the least, and was fully expecting the emails to bounce back. I certainly wasn't expecting to get a reply almost at once. It was from the earwig.net address and it was a very brief reply.

Fuck off.

I put the laptop back in its case, finished my coffee and, feeling extremely deflated, started the engine.

It was only when I was on the road again that it occurred to me that I need not be so downhearted about the response to my email. For a start, I had no idea if it was from the Penelope I'd met last night. Nothing in her attitude to me suggested that she disliked me enough to send me that email. Then again, a complete stranger would almost certainly have either ignored my email or just marked it as spam. True, they might have assumed it was spam and just fired off a reflex response. I'd done that myself a few times with unwanted emails and even the odd unsolicited sales call. But there was a possibility that it was the Penelope I'd met and that somehow I had enraged her.

I didn't really know what to think, but either way, it probably wouldn't be a great idea to email her back straight away, so I decided to think about something else, like getting a new phone. I looked out of the Jag's window to get my bearings and discovered, with a complete lack of surprise, that I was still on the outskirts of Reading. There was a motorway exit coming up, so I took it, and drove into the very heart of Reading.

After a good deal of circling and failed attempts to find a parking space, I decided to head for an enormous multistorey car park in the centre of town, the kind where the pillars are placed too close together and there's always the invisible screech of brakes somewhere above your head. I managed to fit the Jag between two pillars and, avoiding the stinking lift, walked down several flights of steps to a small, depressed shopping centre below. There I managed to buy a pay-as-you-go mobile phone fairly cheaply and without signing a heaving mass of documents. I returned to the Jag, discovered the phone was fully charged and checked my messages.

I had sixteen.

The first message was from Roger Armstrong. I knew it was him because he didn't say his name or anything common like that. He said 'Bread, call me' and rang off.

The second message was also from Roger Armstrong, I'm presuming, because it was just a kind of sighing snort, like a resigned pony might make.

The third, fourth and fifth messages were probably Armstrong, too, as they were the sound of a man ringing off exasperatedly. Again, I'm presuming, because it's hard to detect emotion in someone ringing off, but Armstrong gave it a good go.

The sixth was from Ivor, attempting to check that I was indeed drunk and in the company of a woman called Penelope.

The seventh was from Cora Vanstone.

'This is a message for Charles Bread,' she enunciated, in the cut–glass tones of someone so amazingly posh that they have never had to leave a message of any kind with anyone before. Perhaps leaving voicemail messages was something her butler usually did for her, or her ghillie (I wasn't really sure what a ghillie was, but I bet she had one). 'Please can you call me, Mister Bread, and let me know what your plans are as I have to –'. And then there was the most appalling sound I have ever heard, a noise like a sheet of metal being ripped in half while an animal screamed in terror. Then silence. And then there was a beep and Roger Armstrong said, 'Bread, it would be extremely considerate of you to return my calls at some point today.'

I flicked through the other messages, which were all either Armstrong or spam calls, and then checked to see if voicemail would let me call Cora Vanstone on this phone. It didn't. I sat in the car going through my options for a minute or two – she'd been cut off, the noise was just mobile phone interference, it was unlikely that her house was being bombed or whatever that noise was – before deciding that the only thing I could do in the circumstances was to drive to Devon to Cora Vanstone's house which was, obviously, what I was supposed to be doing in the first place.

Before I did that, I realised, I had better call Roger Armstrong.

'Oh, it's you, Bread.'

I decided to play it dry. 'I think you left a message for me, Roger.'

'Yes. Yes, I did leave a message for you.' Armstrong was laying on the sarcasm now.

'Well,' I said, avoiding any form of apology because, rule one, never apologise to toffs and because an apology would involve some kind of explanation and, rule two, never explain anything to a toff because they will get bored the moment you start talking and cut you off, 'here I am.'

'Good,' said Armstrong. 'Have you heard from Cora Vanstone at all, Bread?'

'Yes,' I said, 'she left a message asking where I was. But it was a bit weird, Roger, and I'm actually quite –'

'I'm not surprised she was asking where you were,' said Armstrong, cutting me off. 'A lot of people are wondering where you are, Bread. It doesn't take long to get from London to Devonshire.'

'I think most people call it Devon now,' I said, which I knew would annoy him, but hey, one–all in my book, and better than telling him that it actually does take long to get to Devon from London, unless you use the secret private jet lane that only the artistocracy know about. 'I was delayed, Roger. I'm back on the road now.'

'I see,' said Armstrong. 'Well, get a move on. There've been developments.'

'What kind of developments?' I said.

'Buy a newspaper,' said Armstrong, curtly. 'A proper one,' he added, and rang off.

In his absence, I swore at my phone for one minute and fifteen seconds and then, much against my better judgement, got out of the car again and went to a newsagent. I got back into the car and opened the newspaper. As it was a *Daily Telegraph* and about the size of a child's bed, I got out of the car again, unfolded it on the roof of the Jag and began to read it. After a minute or so, I found what I presumed I was looking for. An article about copyright law, illustrated with a picture of Peter Pan. According to the piece, something called the Copyright Designs and Patents Act of 1988 was about to be amended to keep up to date with changes in electronic media and blah and blah, which was all fair enough and well and good, but there was some excitement in the air as lawyers for a 'very large international company', whose identity was not revealed but which was strongly hinted at, were protesting at one particular clause in the Act.

The Copyright Designs and Patents Act of 1988 was in line with most worldwide copyright legislation in conferring rights and royalties in a work up to seventy years after the death of the author of the work. What made the Act unique was a clause inserted by former UK Prime Minister James Callaghan – apparently at the insistence of his wife Audrey – which made an exception for *Peter Pan*. All monies and income from *Peter Pan* in the UK were bequeathed to the Great Ormond Street Children's Hospital by JM Barrie in 1937 and – thanks to the Callaghans – this arrangement was enshrined in British law forever. But now lawyers for the unnamed company were arguing that, with Britain's changed status in Europe and so on and so forth, such a clause constituted a restricted practice, was unconstitutional (the UK doesn't have a constitution but there you go) and unfair on, well, large companies who might seek to adapt *Peter Pan* for stage, screen and tablet.

The article didn't make it clear if this was at all likely, but it did point out that, if the law were amended, then there would be a massive upswing in worldwide interest in anything JM Barrie had written. Which, as I had no doubt Armstrong was thinking, would itself stimulate interest in anything JM Barrie might have written. Like, for example, *The Young Visiters*.

If I hadn't felt pressured before – and to be honest, I hadn't, that's not really me – then now I actually was starting to feel pressured.

What had begun as a slight novelty situation, where I'd assumed the odd collector might be curious as to the provenance of a once–beloved children's book, was now turning into something else. Something involving money.

If my instincts led me to believe that the Ashford manuscript had been written by JM Barrie (as it were: a handwriting expert would probably confirm that the words had been dictated by Barrie), then there would be pressure on Pring's: no auction house wants a potentially profitable item to be worthless, so their hopes are all directed at the item being authentic. So if I said it was authentic, a barrier would have been removed to its future sale. But if my instincts (and they were, after all, only instincts) led me to believe that the manuscripts had not been written by Barrie (or worse, had been written by a third party who wasn't even Daisy Ashford), then I might be dealing with a Rawley Vulcan situation again. Pring's would ignore my verbal report, find someone who was able to produce a more amenable report and probably give me the elbow as a liability. I liked my job: I liked the satisfaction of being right, and I liked the money and the Morse Jag.

So the obvious course, if the manuscript wasn't by Barrie, was to lie. To tell Pring's that everything is fine, that the manuscript is by the man who wrote *Peter Pan*, which is about to lose its magic copyright protection, which will mean that many bad men and women will exploit *Peter Pan* for money, which will in turn mean renewed interest in everything else by JM Barrie, which will – according to my lying report – include *The Young Visiters*. Cue profitable movie versions by fashionable directors, cue reprints, pastiches and maybe even apps and games. And cue the appearance of the Ashford Manuscripts at auction, with a new name – the Barrie Manuscripts – and a new, hefty price tag.

It all seemed pretty simple. After all, I'd kept my mouth shut about the Vulcan. True, I hadn't actually *lied* – on the contrary, I'd been completely candid about my findings, it was Armstrong who'd done the actual lying – but I had colluded in the deception. So it shouldn't be too hard to lie about the manuscript. After all, it was only a bit of old paper. Whoever had written *The Young Visiters* – JM Barrie, Daisy

Ashford, Francis Bacon – was long dead, and the book was the same, whoever had written it, wasn't it?

Well, a voice inside me said, a pretty annoying voice if you ask me, *no*. The power of *The Young Visiters* resides to a large extent in the fact that it was written by a nine–year–old girl. It is unique. Attempts to copy it have always failed – Ring Lardner's parody, *The Young Immigrunts*, is good, but is shot through with a wink that says, 'A grown-up wrote this.' There's no such wink in *The Young Visiters*. Its unintentional humour, its charm and its utter lack of tweeness and – I don't know – ick, only work when you know a child wrote those words. It's not important in the bigger scheme of things but then, what is?

You may gather from this that I had not been entirely unaffected by my work here. I had downloaded and read *The Young Visiters,* initially for purely professional reasons, sifting its prose for indicators of an adult hand or to compare it with other works by Barrie (jury still out on both counts). But as I read on – probably around the time the phrase 'on account of the drains in this house' occurred – I started to like it. I laughed a bit. I – and this is the worst part – engaged with the book. I wanted to know about Daisy Ashford. I even ordered a couple of books about her from Abebooks. (Meanwhile, the JM Barrie biographies I'd also bought remained untouched, as did various versions of *Peter Pan*, which I suspected I'd have to be threatened with a cattle prod to go anywhere near.)

I had, unfortunately for me, emotionally invested in the book, and therefore the case. I found myself wanting Daisy Ashford to have written *The Young Visiters*, and not JM Barrie. And why not? Daisy had written only one classic (her other infant works, *Love And Marriage* and *Where Love Lies Deepest*, while sweet, are nothing like *The Young Visiters*) while JM Barrie – well, he too had written only one classic, but that wasn't the point. Thanks to *Peter Pan*, he was everywhere, while Daisy was all but forgotten.

Oh God, I had become a fan of the very thing I was seeking to undermine. Worse, my job was dependent on me destroying the reputation of the very person whose work I suddenly admired. It was like I was a huge Shakespeare fan who had been tasked with proving that

Frances Bacon had written *Hamlet*. Well, not quite like that, because Shakespeare would always be indestructible. But Daisy Ashford...

I liked to think of myself as the Antiques Whisperer, the man who sought out the truth about the past. In reality, I was just a grubby mercenary whose sole contribution to the past would be to consign a nine–year–old girl's one achievement to it.

I was just about to settle into a glum fug for the rest of my journey when my phone rang.

'I need to talk to you,' said Penelope. 'Pull over in that lay–by.'

CHAPTER THREE

'Police estimate the street value of two hundred kilos of cocaine handed into them by Exeter man Giles Wilson as being in the region of two million pounds. "I'm stunned," said Mister Wilson, "We've had it in the family for years and never thought it was worth anything."'

– *Weekending*

'Penelope?' I said, but she was gone. I looked around wildly for another car or perhaps a helicopter but there was nothing. It was a clear stretch of road – clear, except for a lay–by with a sandwich van in it and a trestle table festooned with Saint George flags and selling cherries like there was some connection between cherries and being a bit too keen about England. I nearly overshot the lay–by but managed to pull in at the last minute, sadly not overturning the nationalist cherry stall, and – ignoring the curses of the ruddy-faced stallholder – reversed back to a safer position.

I sat in the car for fully ten minutes. Then, realising I was bored as well as curious, I got out and went to the sandwich stall.

'I'd like a coffee please,' I said to the owner.

'Four pounds,' he replied.

'For a coffee?' I said.

'Two coffees,' he said, nodding back over his shoulder. I looked up, and there on a tree-laden verge behind the van, holding a large coffee, was Penelope.

I paid for the coffees and walked up the verge. Penelope shaded her eyes and grinned at me.

'Bet you didn't expect to see me here,' she said.

'I didn't expect to see you full stop,' I replied. 'Not after that email.'

'What email?' she said.

I took out my phone and showed her. 'Greg,' she said. 'What an arsehole. I'm so sorry. He must have been reading my emails.'

I didn't know what to say. My mind was flipping through options like a Rolodex full of things not to say – *are you sharing an email account? why does he have access to your emails? are you married? do you love him?* – so in the end I said nothing. She must have sensed my confusion – and by 'sensed' I mean 'been able to see it from space' – because she said: 'I left my laptop open when I was working. Greg came in to look at his tweets and the tosser has a habit of snooping. I am really sorry, honest.'

She patted the grass next to her. I sat down, feeling annoyed at myself for clearly initiating a sulk.

'I'm sorry,' I said. 'It threw me for a loop, rather.'

'It what?' she said. 'Threw you what?' And she stared at me. I stared back, for a second. Then I couldn't help it. I started laughing. And she started laughing.

We sat there for a minute or two, waiting for the laughter to subside, until in the end the owner of the cherry stall stomped up to me and said, 'Are you going to move your car? My cherries are blocked in,' and then we completely lost it.

A few minutes later, apologies made to the cherry stall owner, I was driving again and Penelope was in the passenger seat.

'The famous Jag,' she said.

'It's not mine,' I said.

'I know,' said Penelope. 'You explained all that in some detail in the pub, remember?'

'No,' I said, truthfully. 'Thanks for calling Ivor, by the way. I think he liked you.'

'Yeah,' said Penelope, matter-of-factly, 'That happens.'

There was silence in the Jag for a moment. Penelope broke it by rifling through the carrier bag in the passenger footwell.

'Oh my god,' she said, 'These are cassettes.'

'The Jag only plays cassettes,' I explained.

'John Peel 23.8.79,' she read. 'My brother used to tape those shows.'

She looked at me like – well, like an expert might look at a forgery.

'My brother's fifty-six,' she said. 'You're not old enough to have made these.'

I took a deep breath.

'I'm waiting,' she said. 'I want to know.'

'Before I explain,' I said, '*if* I explain… I want you to tell me what you were doing on a grass verge in a lay–by. And how you could see me.'

'That was easy,' she said. 'I've been following you.'

'You what?' I said, narrowly missing a weird French van.

'Well, not intentionally,' she said. 'But I was in my friend Sarah's car and I saw you pull into that pub place back there.'

'The Three For One?' I said. 'But that was hours ago.'

'I know,' Penelope said with feeling. 'My friend Sarah is very angry with me now. I made her wait while you were in there, and again when you were in the Little Chef, and then in Reading…'

'You followed me to *Reading*?'

'Why not? I had nothing else to do. Sarah did, I suppose, which is why she was so angry. But I said I'd babysit for her next week when she wanted to go out with her friends from the stables. And she said I could piss off, which is when I told her to overtake you and drop me in the lay–by.'

With that, Penelope turned a beatific smile on me.

'Now,' she said, before I could ask her if she'd ever been the subject of an exclusion order, 'tell me about the tapes.'

'Later,' I said. 'First I have to get some lunch.'

I can be quite masterful when I want to be, although Penelope was silent for the rest of the drive. Perhaps she was hungry too.

As it turned out, Penelope was very hungry. Fortunately we were in a Humdinger Diner, which is like an American diner if America had lost the War of Independence. Everything on the menu was nominally the kind of food they served in 1950s teen movies – burgers, fries, milk shakes, sodas, that kind of thing – but cooked in an entirely British way. The fries were, essentially, just chips. The burger rolls were baps. The milkshakes were thinly insipid. And the burgers were hard and sharp edged and tasted of shoes.

Despite all this, Penelope ate like she'd recently been given a stomach. She ate all her meal – a substantial Over Easy Pancake Special with rock-hard fried eggs and a pancake that you could have staunched a bleeding wound with – and then started on mine before ordering two banana milkshakes and drinking both of them.

'I needed that,' she said.

'I can see.'

'Now tell me about the tapes,' she said.

'Why?' I said. I could see why her friend Sarah had agreed to drive her for two hours. The woman was relentless.

'Because it's interesting,' said Penelope.

I wriggled slightly in my seat. 'It's actually hard for me to talk about,' I said.

'And that's why it's interesting,' she said. And grinned.

I was about to say something back when I noticed two people sitting at a table by the window. They were the two men from the Three For One Inn and they were studiously pretending not to have seen me.

'We have to go,' I said.

'But I want you to tell me about –'

'Now,' I said, and got up.

To her credit, Penelope didn't ask questions. She followed me as I paid quickly and headed for the car.

As I got in the Jag, I looked back at the Humdinger. The two men were still sitting there. I started the engine and we roared out of the car park.

'Wow,' said Penelope, 'you really don't want to talk about those tapes.'

As the Jag cruised along, I couldn't help wondering what was going on. Were the two men from Humdinger Diner actually following me? I supposed it was possible that they hadn't eaten at the Three For One Inn so had decided to try elsewhere but it was a bit unlikely. Then again it was a bit unlikely that I would end up driving around with a woman I'd only met the night before, so who knew. Perhaps the two men were food critics, visiting all the diners and roadside inns around the South West. Perhaps they were spies for a rival auction house, keen to –

I stopped. This was actually a possibility. I was after all on a mission of some importance. Maybe the two men were from – I didn't know – a foreign company keen to get in on the JM Barrie action early. Maybe they had an expert of their own, ready to step in and tell Cora Vanstone that her manuscript wasn't actually Barrie but they'd take it off her hands as a curio and see what they could do, before selling it in Europe or America as the real deal.

True or not, I had to get a move on. 'Excuse me,' I said to Penelope, and speakerphone–dialled Cora Vanstone. I got an alarming message with the same content as before.

'That doesn't sound good,' said Penelope. 'Not a friend of yours, I hope?'

'A client,' I said, hoping not to explain more.

'Oh, that's right,' she said, 'you're the Antique Whiskerer.'

'The what?' I replied wittily.

'Well, that's what it sounded like last night when you'd had three pints,' said Penelope. 'To be honest, I was quite confused.'

There was nothing for it. Without giving too much away about my current mission, I told Penelope what I did for a living, laying particular emphasis on the discredited Lawrence of Arabia manuscript and not mentioning the Rawley Vulcan at all.

'Oh wow,' she said, even sounding interested. 'So you're the one they call in on *Antiques Roadshow* when they've got some gammy Rembrandt or whatever.'

'Not exactly,' I said. 'But close enough.'

'And this client you're going to see, the one who sounds like she's being murdered,' said Penelope tastefully. 'Has she got a gammy Rembrandt?'

'We'll see,' I said, and moved into the middle lane. I don't like to make a show of myself.

'I don't wish to be rude,' I said, half an hour later, 'but why, you know, are you here?'

'That is a bit rude,' said Penelope. 'I'm bored, I suppose. Bored of Greg. Bored of sitting at home waiting for him to call and tell me he's on his way down from London. Bored of never doing anything. Sarah's all right but she's got three kids and a dog and that's all she ever talks about. And then here you are with your Jag and your antique whiskering and it's all fairly entertaining.'

She paused and, in a different tone, said, 'You can let me out here if you like.'

'I didn't mean that,' I said, 'It's just –'

'No, it's fine. Just by the roundabout will do.'

'I didn't mean to offend you.'

'I'm not offended. Just here is fine.'

'I can't drop you by a roundabout.'

'Do you have a piece of old cardboard? I can write a sign and hitch back home.'

'I – no, I don't have a piece of old cardboard. Look, I want you to stay, okay?'

'Good.'

'All right.'

'There's the exit for the M3.'

'I saw it.'

'I'm sure you did.'

The M3 was very slow. Cars moved forwards a few yards, slowed down, stopped, then moved forwards again. The fast lane was immobile and the slow lane full of container trucks, double–decker coaches and vehicle transporters. I stayed in the middle lane, trapped between a Ford Ka impossibly crammed with lads and a huge Land Rover driven by a tiny glamour model.

Penelope was sifting through my tapes again, reading out the titles in the voice of a BBC announcer.

'John Peel 14.5.83… John Peel 6.9.97… Ooh, this one's from 2000, I might know some of these songs.'

'Put that back.'

'Why? I want some music and I'm not listening to the radio, it's awful.'

'Put it back. I have – a system.'

Penelope looked at me. 'You're getting weirder by the second.'

'I'm not. It's just – I like to know what tapes I've played.'

'Well,' she said, a little heavily. 'This one is from June 2000.'

'Don't tell me,' I said. 'I want it to be a surprise.'

Penelope looked at me again. 'You want what to be a surprise?'

'I can't tell you.'

'You can't tell me what?'

'Can you just let me choose the tapes please?'

'Okay. All right. Which one do you want?'

'It doesn't work like that. You just have – can you take one out and put in the player please without –'

'Without telling you what it is?'

'Yes. I'm sorry, I know it sounds weird –'

'Not at all.'

'– but I have a system.'

Penelope sighed, ejected the previous cassette, rummaged for a fresh tape and put it in the player. I exhaled.

'Thank you,' I said.

'You're welcome, she said.

'*...And last night I played you a French single featuring Joy Division on the Sordide Sentimentale label, and I promised to play the other side of it tonight, and indeed I shall. In fact, I shall do it right now...*'

Joy Division's 'Dead Souls', framed in tape hiss, filled the car. Penelope looked out the window. The car in front slowed to a standstill. I turned on the air con. She turned it off.

A few minutes passed in this companionable silence until suddenly Penelope said, 'They're behind us.'

'Who are?' I said, but I knew.

'Those men from the diner. I saw you looking at them earlier. They were in the diner, not eating anything, and they're behind us.'

'Where?' I said.

'Use the mirrors and don't turn your head. Three cars behind us in the fast lane, in the white Prius.'

I looked in the rear–view mirror. She was right. Both of them, sitting in the front seats of a new Toyota. They hadn't seen me looking as they were too busy messing about with a satnav which had apparently fallen off its mount.

'I wonder what they want,' Penelope said and then, as the traffic briefly lurched forward, 'It's hardly a high–speed chase, is it?'

I kept an eye on the two men in the Toyota. They didn't seem to be looking our way but then if they were following us, they wouldn't want to attract our attention. We sat in traffic, the heat of the day rising. There was a faint shimmer on the central reservation. A white butterfly landed on some dandelions.

'People say that you never see any good butterflies these days,' said Penelope.

'I suppose not,' I said. 'But then we're hardly spoilt for choice are we? I mean there's the –'

I stopped, suddenly aware that I didn't know the names of any butterflies.

'Red Admiral?' said Penelope, 'Tortoiseshell? Peacock?'

'Yes,' I said. 'Those ones. That's all of them, isn't it? Apart from that white one.'

'That's not true,' she said, with surprising vigour. 'Only the other day, I saw…' she paused for dramatic effect, 'a Camberwell Beauty.'

'Really?' I said. 'I've never heard of it.'

'Wow,' she said, and turned to look out of the window. That's the thing about women. One minute they're impressed about your collection of old radio shows and the next they're miffed because you don't know anything about butterflies.

Penelope turned back to me. She seemed less annoyed. 'I suppose working for an auction house there isn't much call for knowing about butterflies.'

'Not really,' I said. 'I can't think of a single situation where being an expert on –'

'Lepidoptera.'

'That. Would come in handy,' I agreed.

'I belonged to a book club once,' said Penelope, out of nowhere.

'I see,' I said, not seeing.

'We couldn't agree on what books to read. It's a small village, but it's amazing how much variation in people's reading tastes there can be.'

'I thought that was the point of a book club,' I said, wondering what the hell we were talking about.

'Someone wanted to talk about *Fifty Shades of Grey*, but the vicar wasn't having it – she wanted us to read some woman who wrote about World War One, someone else only liked Agatha Christie, and I couldn't think of anything,' Penelope continued. 'In the end, I saw this book on the shelf. *The Little Book of Butterflies and Moths*. So I suggested we all read that instead.'

'And did you?'

'Yes. And do you know what? It turns out that people have strong views on butterflies and moths. Really strong views.'

'I find that hard to believe.'

'All right. One simple question. Which do you like best, butterflies or moths?'

To my surprise, I found I was giving the question serious thought. 'Moths.'

'*Moths?*'

'Yeah, why not?'

'Most people say butterflies.'

'Well, I'm saying moths. I like moths. Moths are – well, they're...' I stopped. I could not for the life of me think why I liked moths.

'Moths are creepy,' said Penelope. 'They live in the dark and there's the whole lightbulb thing. And they've got skulls on their backs like Nazis. Moths are Nazis.'

'That's a bit extreme,' I said. 'Besides, butterflies are show-offs. All that colour and being shiny. No, give me a moth any day.'

'So what's your favourite moth?'

Now it was my turn to grin. 'I don't have a favourite moth,' I said. 'That would be like me asking you what your favourite butterfly was.'

Penelope looked at me. 'That's easy,' she said. 'The Camberwell Beauty.' At that moment, whatever was causing the traffic jam up ahead unblocked itself, the cars began to move again and we started to pick up pace.

'Turn off there,' said Penelope. There was an exit sign ahead.

'Why?' I said. 'It's the middle of nowhere.'

'But we can lose them,' she said. I looked in the rear-view mirror. The Toyota had its indicators on and was clearly about to follow us.

'I'm not sure we will,' I said.

'Just do it,' she said. I crossed into the slow lane and headed for the exit. As I did so, the Toyota followed.

And then, as we were about a metre from the exit, Penelope grabbed the steering wheel and yanked the car back into the lane again, narrowly missing a little purple car. She jerked the wheel again and this time we slid into the middle lane, and then the fast lane. Cars all around us were honking wildly.

'Are you mad?' I said, regaining control of the Jag.

'Maybe,' she said, 'but we've lost those two.'

I looked across the road. The Toyota, forced to take the exit, was now circling a roundabout and trying to find its way back onto the motorway.

'Put your foot down,' said Penelope.

I did so.

The Jag was making good time now, so it was annoying to say the least when I looked at the petrol gauge and saw that it was pretty close to zero.

'We need to find a service station,' I said.

'I know a place,' said Penelope. 'You won't like it, though.'

'The service station or the place?' I said.

'You'll see,' she said. 'Take the next junction. No, the one after that.'

Soon we were in one of those bizarre whirlpools of roundabouts which seem to infest the south of England, each roundabout leading to a mile or so of road which in turn leads to another roundabout, which leads to another roundabout, and so on, the tarmac equivalent of those crop circles which were so popular a decade or two back. I was just starting to get dizzy with the constant left turns and sudden exits when Penelope sat up and said, 'There it is.'

I looked up and there it was. A forest of biscuit-coloured stone, at once remarkable and bland. It was half a Regency crescent grown bloated beyond recognition and half mutant Tesco superstore. Cranes speckled the air, suggesting that it was growing to fill the available countryside, while vans dotted in and out of it like drones bringing food to some hideous monster hive.

'Oh my god,' I said. 'Poundbury.'

'I knew you wouldn't like it,' Penelope said.

'Like it?' I said. 'I *love* it. I've always wanted to come here.'

'You're weird,' said Penelope as we turned off the main road and headed for the exit.

I wasn't joking, either. Other people want to go to India or climb Mount Everest. My ambition has always been to visit Poundbury. I don't know why I've never got around to it. I suppose I was always putting it off for a special occasion. Or maybe I just feared disappointment. You can build things up in your mind too much sometimes.

Poundbury has always occupied a special place in my heart. Whenever my dad took me and my mum on holiday, we always had to drive past Poundbury. I would gaze out of the car window as its Georgian houses, peasant barns and Toytown shops went up, bit by bit, and wonder what it was. Poundbury is that rarest thing in the twenty-first century, the product of one man's vision. These days, making anything new is generally the job of huge corporations, but Poundbury is exceptional because it was devised and built in unique circumstances.

To construct a village in modern times, you need to own a large tract of land, to have access to a team of architects and to be free of planning restrictions. It also helps to be heir to a throne. His Royal Highness Prince Charles ticks all those boxes, and also possesses the necessary grit in the oyster of his ambition (if you see what I mean). For a long time, Charles has been publicly opposed to modernism, brutalism and pretty much every other architectural ism. He famously called London's South Bank Centre a 'carbuncle' and has himself been accused of being out of date and out of touch.

Other people have disliked modern architecture but very few of them have been able to actually do anything about it. Charles was different: he commissioned Poundbury as a way of putting his money where his mouth is. Designed by sympathetic architects, built according to a vision of a lost, arguably non-existent England, Poundbury for many is an ideal for living, a community untouched by the drab greyness of modern building.

As we drove in, I felt a frisson of excitement. Still uncompleted,

Poundbury is a quiet place. There are, by design, few cars, and in the middle of a working day, Poundbury was like a film set of a Wild West town. I almost expected some townsfolk to run for cover in a nearby saloon as we passed. There even was a saloon, of sorts, a huge pub called The Poet Laureate, its sign a large portrait of the late Ted Hughes. It looked friendly, if slightly unreal, so I suggested to Penelope that we take a look.

We parked and walked through the village, past Victorian cottages that were less than a decade old, down pavements lined with young trees, and were even overtaken by some children on bicycles, their satchels presumably containing bottles of fizzy pop and sherbert dib-dabs.

'This is weird,' said Penelope.

'I know,' I said.

'Look at that house,' Penelope said, pointing at a pillar-studded edifice. 'It's like something out of Jane Austen.'

I nodded in agreement. 'Prince Charles said he wanted to build a model village,' I replied, 'and I think he did in more than one sense of the word.'

'You're right,' she said. 'I keep expecting giant people to lean in and point at us.'

'There's the pub,' I said, and we crossed the empty road to The Poet Laureate. As we did so, I looked up, half expecting huge fingers to reach down and pluck us up into the sky.

'Two pints of Otter,' Penelope said to the landlord.

'I'm driving,' I said.

'You can have a pint,' she said, paying for the drinks.

'Is there a petrol station near here?' I asked the landlord.

'Petrol station?' he said, and laughed, as though I'd asked him if there was a giant ocelot near here. 'No, there isn't. Not allowed, you see.'

'Of course,' I said, resisting the urge to ask what time curfew was. We sat down with our drinks.

'This reminds me of something,' said Penelope. 'That old TV series.'

'Narrows it down,' I said.

'You know what I mean,' she said. 'The one they filmed in that village. Portmeirion.'

'*The Prisoner*,' I replied. 'Although this place is kind of the anti-Portmeirion. Because that was one man's vision but –'

'Clough Williams-Ellis,' she said, 'and it's different because it's frivolous and whimsical where this is meant to be functional.'

She gave me one of her looks again. This one felt like a small drill.

'Oh fuck,' she said.

'What?' I said.

Penelope nodded her head almost imperceptibly at the window. The two men from the Three For One Inn were crossing the road.

'Let's get out of here,' I suggested.

'I've got a better idea,' said Penelope, and went up to the bar. She exchanged a few words with the landlord and returned to her seat.

'Enjoy your pint,' she said as the men entered and went up to the bar. To my surprise, the landlord immediately engaged them in animated conversation. The men kept looking over at our table, but the landlord wouldn't let them go. Soon he was drawing them small glasses of ale and pushing menus at them.

'What the hell is going on?' I said.

'I told the landlord that they were from the *Good Food Guide*,' said Penelope. 'I said I'd seen them in Dorchester talking about how they were coming here with a view to awarding it a rosette.'

'What?' I said. 'Really?'

'Of course not,' she said. 'I told him those men were following us and could he stall them for a couple of minutes. Now drink up and let's get out of here.'

We finished our drinks and left the two men stuck at the bar.

After driving for a few minutes, I found a petrol station and filled the Jag up.

'Now what?' said Penelope as I nosed the Jag into yet another B-road.

'Well, I'm going to Devon,' I said. 'You're welcome to join me, but it won't be very interesting.'

'Right,' said Penelope. 'You're engaged in a task so dull that two men are following you. Not that you've told me anything about it.'

'Client confidentiality,' I said.

'Cobblers,' she said. 'After all I've done for you, you owe me.'

'All right,' I said and told her the whole story, from Cora Vanstone's letter to the business with the *Peter Pan* copyright.

'Blimey,' said Penelope, 'and you've not seen this document yourself?'

'Only a copy,' I said, 'which for my purposes isn't enough.'

'I know,' she said, 'you have to sniff the paper and hold it up to the light and all that... I'm not taking the mickey, I'm just saying that's what you do.'

'It's a little more complicated than that,' I said.

'Is it?' she said, grinning again.

'Perhaps not,' I admitted. 'Will you leave those tapes alone?'

But Penelope was already rooting through the carrier bag.

'Peel Show 23.11.98,' she read, 'Peel Show 17.5.79... these are all so *random.*'

'Please put those back,' I said.

'I am,' she said. 'I don't want to interfere with your precious *system.* Although how you can call playing tapes at random a system beats –'

She stopped. She was looking at the label on a cassette.

'Wait a minute,' she said, 'this one says *Perfumed Garden* 14.8.67.'

'Please put it back,' I said, tersely. 'And stop reading the names out. I told you, I don't like to know the names.'

'67,' she said, ignoring me. '1967. Most people didn't have cassettes in 1967. But this is – they all are. They're all on the same kind of cassette.'

'Are they?' I said. 'I hadn't noticed.'

'All of them,' said Penelope. 'The '70s ones, the '90s ones, they're all on the same make of cassette. That's impossible. I mean, if they're the original tapes.'

'How mysterious,' I said. 'Can you check something on the satnav for me?'

'No,' she said. 'Not until you tell me why all these tapes are the same.'

I sighed. 'All right,' I said. 'They're all on the same kind of tapes because they're not the real tapes.'

'What do you mean they're not the real tapes?'

'I mean, they're the real shows, the ones that were broadcast, but they're not original tapes. Not all of them.'

'I knew that,' she said. 'Like I say, you're not old enough to have recorded them at the time. And also like I said, who had cassettes in 1967?'

'You're right. They're not all tapes from the time because I didn't record all of them at the time,' I said.

'Then what did you do?' said Penelope, sounding resigned to this line of inquiry.

'I... I downloaded them.'

'What, from the internet? Can you do that?'

'Oh yes. There are whole websites of Peel shows. People archive them and put them up so other people can play them. All you need is a bit of semi-legal software and you can download them.'

'But these aren't, what is it, MP3s or files. They're tapes.'

'I know,' I said. 'But I like tapes. I like the idea of them, and the feel. And –'

'And what?' said Penelope.

'I like the fakeness of doing this. Of taking something that was originally recorded on a radio, late at night, with crackling static, maybe even under a blanket, or with headphones on, that's been transferred digitally, and then I download it and put it back on tape. It's like a perfect recreation. An almost untraceable forgery.'

There was silence in the car again.

'Do you think I'm a bit weird?' I said.

'Do you have to ask?' said Penelope.

'They're not all downloads,' I said, digging my grave of shame deeper with my shovel of embarrassment.

She looked at me.

'I also buy random collections of cassettes online,' I said. 'Which I then...'

'Oh god,' she said, 'which you then what?'

'Digitise,' I said. 'So I can play them on my computer.'

'You are a bit weird,' she said, and reached into the bag again. 'Festive Fifty –' she began.

'What?' I said urgently.

'Jesus, don't bite my head off,' said Penelope. 'What's a Festive Fifty?'

'Nothing,' I said. 'Doesn't matter.'

'Shall I put it back?' she said.

There was a sticky silence.

'What year is it?' I said.

'What, now?' she said.

'No, what year is the Festive Fifty? On the tape.'

She looked at the cassette.

'2008,' she said. 'Why?'

I didn't reply. She already thought I was insane. Why make it worse?

'Weirdo,' she said, and put the tape on.

'*And that's at number 24 in the Festive Fifty, Shotgun Funeral by The Party of One, seven–inch single on FatCat Records. And in case anybody's thinking of writing to us or emailing us or writing a newspaper piece to the effect that most of the records so far seem to be by cute white kids strumming guitars – this is always the case, and it's not my choice, it's yours.*'

Peel sounded embattled. I knew how he felt.

After a few miles, Penelope nodded off. I turned down the Peel tape – after all, there are only so many cute white kids strumming guitars that anyone can take – and looked at the satnav. With reasonable traffic speeds, we could be in Budleigh Salterton in less than two hours. I still didn't know what I was going to do about, or indeed, with Penelope. I doubted she would want to wait in the car while I had a look at Cora Vanstone's document. I imagined that she would probably pretend to be my assistant or possibly even make me pretend to be her assistant. Either way, I wouldn't be bored.

I looked over at her. I wasn't what you would call a ladies' man. I wasn't really an anyone's man, frankly. Yet here I was, driving across England, with an attractive woman who had met me less than twenty-four hours ago and was prepared to go adventuring with me.

I wasn't sure about the word adventuring, but given we had been followed, it seemed right to use that word.

At that moment, my phone rang. I recognised the number. Roger Armstrong. With a low sigh, I put it on speaker.

'Bread,' said Armstrong. 'Where the hell are you?'

'Good to hear from you, Roger,' I said, as Penelope let out a snore of equine proportions. 'I'm still motoring across Dorset.'

'Dorset?' he said, as though I had told him I was motoring across Mordor. 'You should be in East Devon by now.'

'Had a few issues with the Jag,' I said.

'Get a proper car,' he said curtly. 'Now listen, Bread, I'm on the train. I need to see you.'

'Everything's under control,' I said.

'I doubt that,' Armstrong said. 'Meet me in one hour. Exeter St Davids.'

'Could you at least tell me –' I said, but, having delivered instructions to a serf, Armstrong was gone. I sighed, and reached for the satnav. It fell off the windscreen into my lap and Penelope woke up.

'What's going on?' she said.

'I have to meet my boss,' I explained.

'Who's your boss?'

'He's called Roger Armstrong. Not a nice man.'

There was a pause while Penelope assimilated this change of plans. She didn't seem very happy about it. But then, nor did I.

'Why are you meeting him?'

'No idea.'

'Okay… where are you meeting him?'

I told her.

'Doesn't that take us out of our way?'

I noted the 'our' but said nothing. 'It does. Like I said, he's my boss.'

'I don't like it.'

'Me neither. I've come all this way and I hope he's not telling me to jack it in.'

Penelope sighed.

'Right, give me that thing.'

I pulled the satnav away from the windscreen and Penelope began resetting it.

An hour later, we were in Exeter. I have to say, I have never liked Exeter. The cathedral apart, whose flying buttresses were apparently the toast of Europe when they were first unveiled, Exeter is a grim old place, with bits of Tudor guff dotted here and there to conceal the fact that it's a generic kind of place. The city came first a few years ago in a survey of what are known as clone towns, because its main street had more generic shops and stores than anywhere else in Britain. Here, at the university end of town, that effect was less pronounced, in that there were more pubs and takeaways, some of which looked quite good.

We drove downhill and passed the only landmark I had ever liked – a boarding house called the Telstar Hotel, a reminder of a moment of British technological hope that had faded before the owner put the sign up – and circled St Davids Station, looking for a parking spot.

After a few minutes, a large SUV full of blonde children gave up trying to cram itself into a slender parking space and I nudged the Jag in between some sort of white car which looked like a soldier in a *Star Wars* film and an actual tractor.

'Now what?' said Penelope.

'I suppose we wait for his train to get in,' I said.

'Has he told you which one he's on?' she asked.

I gave her my best old-fashioned look.

'Of course not,' I said. 'He was at Marlborough.'

Penelope looked out of the window.

'It's raining,' she said. 'I'm not getting out.'

'Fair enough,' I said. I hadn't been looking forward to meeting Armstrong in the company of a female stranger anyway. He would have been bound to raise, if not an objection, then his eyebrows: at least this way I'd have a few seconds to explain that I had acquired a passenger. Explain, I thought, to myself as well as to him.

I left Penelope in the car and walked through the warm Devon drizzle to the station. In the foyer or whatever it's called, I struggled to find an arrivals board and eventually found one several feet in the air next to a Starbucks. Craning my neck, I could see that Armstrong's train was running late.

I looked out the way I had come. It was now raining quite heavily. I felt bad leaving Penelope on her own for an hour in the car, so I called her to say I'd be coming back to sit with her and did she want a coffee. Her phone went to voicemail, or at least I thought it did, as all I could hear was a muted bleep, as might be made by an unwell robot.

Sighing, I went and got two coffees and headed back to the car. Penelope wasn't in it. The key was still in the ignition, and my bag was still on the back seat but Penelope was gone. I looked around the car park but couldn't see her. She must have got out of the car seconds after I had, and headed straight up the hill. Or sneaked around me into the station and got on a train. Anything was possible.

And one thing was probable. She'd got bored of our escapade and gone back to her village life of, I assumed, affairs with the likes of Greg. I couldn't blame her, to be honest; the adventure so far had largely consisted of driving round some of the duller parts of the West Country with the far-from-exciting promise of a visit to an old lady in Budleigh Salterton to look at some old paper.

At least now, I thought unhappily as I locked the Jag and walked back to the station, I wouldn't have to worry about explaining her to Armstrong.

As it turned out, Armstrong's train was even later than it was officially meant to be, which meant I'd had time to drink both coffees, go to the toilet, buy a copy of *Record Collector* – there was a piece about the Peel Sessions in it – and call Penelope's number five or six times without any luck.

I closed the magazine, put my phone away and looked at my watch just as the tannoy announced the arrival of the train from London Waterloo – as opposed, I remember thinking, to Belgium Waterloo or Abba Waterloo or one of the many other Waterloos. I positioned myself in front of the ticket gate and waited for Armstrong to, I was guessing, saunter like a promenading git without a care in the world towards the exit.

I was wrong. As Armstrong approached the barrier, attaché case and *Financial Times* in hand, I was surprised to see that he appeared quite agitated.

'Hello, Roger,' I said.

'Where's the car?' he replied, all his reserves of old–school–tie charm apparently depleted.

I led him to the car and we got in. I waited to see if he wanted me to start the engine or something crazy like that, but instead he just sat there, breathing loudly through his expensively educated nostrils.

At last he stopped his exhalations and turned to look at me.

'Who are you working for, Bread?' he said.

I was taken aback.

'Well, technically, I'm self-employed so no-one, I suppose,' I began. 'But since Pring's pay me a retainer, and commission... you.'

'This is because of the Rawley business, isn't it?' said Armstrong. 'You've had a down on us ever since you messed up with the Vulcan.'

'I really don't know what you're talking about,' I said. 'And not in the sense of I'm annoyed and denying everything either... I really *really* don't know what you mean.'

'You got a slapped wrist on that one,' said Armstrong. 'I thought I'd taught you a lesson, but no, clearly you bore a grudge and now you've found a way to get back at me.'

'I really don't –' I began, and stopped because I'd just said 'I really don't know what you're talking about' and felt I needed to move on. I took a deep breath. 'Look, I was pretty shaken up by all that and yes, you pissed me off, but I'm still here, I took it all on board, rightly or wrongly, and I'm dealing with it. So whatever you're talking about, it wasn't me,' I said. A moment later, I added, 'What *are* you talking about, by the way?'

By way of answer, Armstrong whacked his *Financial Times* at me. I took it from him and saw that he had folded it open at one page.

'Is this the *Peter Pan* thing?' I said. 'Because –'

'Just read it,' said Armstrong, his nostrils quivering like a Derby winner's.

I looked at the paper. There were, unsurprisingly in the circumstances, a picture of JM Barrie and a picture of the Disney Peter Pan. But next to them, and occupying as much space as the other two pictures put together, was a Victorian photograph of a young girl. Daisy Ashford.

'Oh no,' I said. 'Does this –'

'*Read it,*' said Armstrong, his throat almost twanging with rage.

The piece was actually quite short but it created a rising horror inside me. It said that an unnamed person in the West Country had stumbled across some documents which appeared to be the work of JM Barrie author of blah blah blah and which had previously been attributed to Daisy Ashford youthful author of more blah and blah meaning that said documents were in the light of recent developments worth a great deal money of blah. All of this was bad enough but the piece went on to state that 'the documents have now apparently been confirmed as the work of JM Barrie by an independent investigator working for a major international auction house'.

'But that could be anyone,' I said.

'Yes, any one of the thousands of independent investigators from major international auction houses who know about this,' sneered Armstrong. 'Bread, I checked. No other house knew about this. Not until this fucking story appeared and now I imagine every independent investigator working for a major international auction house is on his way down to Devon.'

'It doesn't mention Cora Vanstone,' I pointed out lamely.

'It doesn't have to. All it takes is one call to the hack who wrote this and her name will be all over Google.'

Slightly impressed that Armstrong had heard of Google, I said, 'You think it was me who told them about the document, don't you?'

'Well, who else could it be? Unless Vanstone lied and she sent the same letter to everyone. Which we both know is unlikely.'

I didn't see why it was unlikely, but decided to say nothing. There was nothing to stop Cora Vanstone writing to every auction house in the land, but equally it made sense for her to approach houses one by one.

'It still wasn't me,' I said. 'I haven't even got to Budleigh Salterton yet.'

'Which in itself is suspicious,' Armstrong said. 'You've had enough time to get there and back. Which for all I know is exactly what you did. Went down to Budleigh Salterton, told the old bat her documents were real, and then buggered off to Dorset and told me you were still on your way... What have you been doing all this time, anyway?'

'I told you,' I said, then realised I couldn't remember what I had told him. 'The Jag broke down and I had to spend the night in a motel and then...'

'I don't want to hear it, Bread,' Armstrong interrupted. 'I don't trust you and I don't like you. But –'

As Armstrong said 'but', I realised that for some reason he had decided to be magnanimous in his own clipped, empty-sanatorium kind of way.

'I can't work out, if you were trying to screw us, why the piece in the paper would attribute the authentication to an independent investigator. It pretty squarely puts the blame on you, from my point of view at least.'

'I suppose so,' I said. 'But why would anyone want to do that? I don't have any enemies. At least –' I added, catching Armstrong's eye, 'not any who could be bothered to do me harm. Nobody cares about me, Armstrong.'

'Nobody did,' he said. 'Until this Barrie business came along. Bread, if these documents turn out to be real, they're going to be very valuable and a lot of people are going to want a piece of them. Unscrupulous people. Bad people.'

'Then how does it help to start a story that I've authenticated them?' I said. 'Surely that just tells the world that Pring's have got to the goods first.'

'You're not getting it,' said Armstrong. 'That story isn't there to make Pring's look good if the documents are real. It's there to make us look bad if they're not real.'

He sat back in his seat, looking exhausted.

'Have you heard from Cora Vanstone at all?' he said.

'No. I left messages but nothing. Do you want to come with me now? We can be there in an hour.'

'Bread, it's half past seven at night and I'm too tired to deal with this now. Besides, if she's seen the paper, she'll be furious. Leave another message and tell her we'll be there in the morning.'

'But what about the piece?'

'Tell her it's made up by our rivals, there's no truth in it and she's not to talk to anyone until we get there. And for God's sake don't mention money. So far as she's concerned, the documents aren't worth anything until our people, and nobody else's, have examined them. Now take me to my hotel.'

'Your hotel?'

'Yes. You can find a B & B or something.'

I drove Armstrong in silence to his hotel and asked the receptionist if he knew any bed and breakfasts nearby. The friendly receptionist googled me a few and I chose the nearest. It wasn't the Telstar but you can't have everything. As I got my stuff out of the Jag, a small piece of yellow paper fluttered out. It was a Post-It note and it must have fallen off the inside of the windscreen. On it were written three words: I'M SORRY – P.

I am not a man given to introspection. I prefer to not so much suffer the slings and arrows of outrageous fortune as let them bounce off me. In times of trouble, I like to imagine that I am surrounded by an invisible forcefield, which is impermeable to insult, emotion and physical pain. Today, however, it seemed that my forcefield was in need of new batteries. Today had been, in a phrase my dad had once used, an absolute shunt-up of a Bulgarian fire drill. I had no idea what a Bulgarian fire drill was, but it seemed apt.

Nothing – literally nothing – had gone right lately. I had been robbed. My car, which wasn't my car, had been vandalised. I had been forced to visit a Three For One Inn. And I had met someone who seemed charming, delightful and – I had dared to think – attracted to me. And now they were gone. Even by the low standards of the average Bulgarian fire drill, today had been entirely appalling.

I screwed up the note and threw it away.

'Oi!' said a voice. I turned to see a fat, angry-looking man with an even fatter, angrier-looking dog.

'Pick that up!' he said, pointing at the paper on the ground.

I pulled a crossbow from under my coat and let him have a bolt between the eyes. Of course I didn't. I picked up the paper, and went inside.

After a breakfast in the bed and breakfast whose one merit had been that it was better than the bed, I walked out in a sunny Exeter morning. I called Armstrong but his phone went straight to voicemail, so I drove to his hotel where I was told by a markedly less friendly receptionist that he had checked out of his room. Nice of him to tell me, I thought, faced with the prospect of wandering around the city all morning waiting for a posh man to call me. I realised that I didn't really have an alternative, other than faking my own death or changing my identity and getting out of the whole business altogether, so I decided to walk towards the only place I knew and liked in town, the cathedral, and delete the awful breakfast from my taste buds by having a coffee in one of the tea rooms in the close.

I found it surprisingly difficult to make my way down the street because there was an early–morning crowd of tourists flumping its way in the same direction. As someone who grew up in a holiday part of the world, I have always had a visceral contempt for tourists. 'Grockles,' they call them in this part of the world, 'emmets' in Cornwall. Despite the fact that people here have always been dependent on tourism for their livelihood, Devonians – like anyone who lives and works in a holiday location – have always had the same attitude to tourists that the population of an invaded country have always had towards the occupying forces. It's a symbiotic relationship, like the one between a hippo and the birds who clean the ticks off its back, except the birds hate the hippo and, presumably, themselves.

This particular crowd of tourists were eminently hateable as, despite being led by a woman with a large plastic Union Jack umbrella, they seemed incapable of moving in a straight line, and as a group would eddy back and forth and even sideways into the road, like a kind of sentient paint spill, looking round them in confusion at every junction and pointing at the most mundane objects, like traffic lights or pushchairs. Several of them were also carrying selfie sticks, in case they saw the Eiffel Tower or the Empire State Building and felt the need to show their friends what a famous landmark would look like with them standing in front of it.

I wondered where they were going, and soon found out. Parked by the side of the road, in a location where a parked bee would have caused a major traffic jam, was a large red double-decker bus, whose roof had been removed. On the side of the bus was an enormous Union Jack and the words EXETOURS. To my immense relief, the tourists were flowing slowly towards this bus, presumably to enjoy a guided tour of the sights of the city.

There seemed however to be a problem. The driver and the fare collector were deep in discussion, in a way that involved them blocking the pavement, because while the fare collector was a slim young woman, the driver was a fat-arse and no mistake.

'He hasn't turned up yet,' said the driver.

'Or she,' said the fare collector, who was clearly a feminist.

'Excuse me,' I said.

'You'll have to wait,' said the driver, mistaking me for a tourist. 'Guide hasn't turned up yet.'

'Wait for what?' I was about to say, when I realised that he had assumed I was waiting to get on his bus for, presumably, a tour of the city – a tour whose thrilling commencement was apparently being delayed by the non-appearance of the tour guide. Normally I would have been offended to be mistaken for a grockle but at that moment I saw them. The two men from the Three For One.

There was no mistaking them and their conspicuous double-actery. The thin one was walking like a flamingo in a hurry, strutting forwards with an air of anorexic urgency, while the round one resembled nothing so much as a sentient chew toy on a mission. And they were coming towards me, looking, in a phrase, pretty hacked off. I could tell they were hacked off because they both looked hacked off and, perhaps more to the point, one of them was reaching into his jacket pocket. Arguably he could have been reaching for some identification, or his phone; on the other hand, he and his associate had been following me for two days now, quite clearly following me.

This had never happened to me before, of course. I was not in the habit of being pursued with evil intent by unusual-looking duos. I wondered what I should do now. For a moment I considered walking over to them and punching one of them right in the nose. I was angry enough. Right then I could have probably taken on both of them, eyes closed, and had the fuckers on the ground before they even saw me coming. Hang the consequences; whatever happened, it would make me feel better. I might even kick one up the arse and pretend it was Armstrong I was kicking, the well-spoken wanker.

But then, at the exact moment I had decided that, yes, it was arse-kicking time, one of the pair reached into his pocket. This stalled me: it was totally possible that he was reaching for his phone, or an ID card, or even a sandwich, but the way things were going right now, who knew?

I looked around. The other direction was still blocked by the driver and the ticket collector, who were obviously stymied by the non-arrival of the tour guide – I made a decision. It wasn't the sort of decision I'd normally make, but maybe I had learned recklessness from Penelope or possibly I was just panicking and desperate, I didn't know.

'Excuse me,' I said again to the driver, 'but I am the tour guide.'

'What?' he said.

'You heard him,' said the fare collector. 'You're late,' she said to me and actually handed me a peaked cap.

'Sorry,' I said and jumped aboard. I could still see the two men pushing their way through the melee of tourists as I rapidly climbed the stair to the open top deck. As the passengers followed me and began to fill the tour bus's seats, I was able to take stock of my plan. It was very simple: I hadn't got one.

I was just wondering if I could feign a stomach ache and hop off at the next lights when the two men from the Three For One appeared at the top of the stair and sat down on each side of the aisle. Now, unless I jumped off the bus into a passing haycart, there was no way out.

There was a ding from below. The bus pulled out into the light morning traffic. The fare collector had appeared by my side to hand me a large cordless microphone.

'Not the usual lot,' she said. 'Dutch or Belgian.'

I looked at my audience. Forty or so expectant Dutch or Belgians, keen to learn more about Devon's second–largest city. And, at the back of the bus, two men who clearly wanted to have a chat with me. There was, as I said, no way out.

I tapped the microphone.

'Testing,' I said. 'Testing. One, two, three.'

One of the two men at the back raised an eyebrow. The other looked at me and fingered his jacket pocket meaningfully. Everyone else just looked slightly bovine.

'Hello and welcome to, to today's tour,' I said. 'We will be passing through this wonderful old city of Exeter and its environs –'

The fare collector shook her head.

'– through the centre of this wonderful old city,' I said, 'and examining a hundred years of history.'

Again she shook her head.

'Five hundred years –'

Now she looked annoyed.

'A thousand years of history,' I said, disbelievingly.

'Wow, that's a lot of history!' said one of the Dutch or Belgians, nudging his companion heftily.

'Too right,' I said. The fare collector was giving me a distinctly primeval look now, so I turned my head to see that we were heading for the railway station, St Davids, the one I'd come into last night.

'This is Exeter St Davids station,' I said, accurately, secure for a moment in the knowledge at least that I'd started on the right foot. 'It was –'

I racked my mind for anything I knew about the station. And then I remembered.

'It was built to service the Great Western Railway in the year, in the nineteenth century,' I said confidently, 'and as such will have played host to Sir Isambard Kingdom Brunel, the greatest engineer this country has ever known.'

As I emptied out my limited store of facts about Sir Isambard Kingdom Brunel, the fare collector, presumably inured to this sort of historical logorrhoea, went back downstairs. This was fortunate because I was running out of facts about Sir Isambard Kingdom Brunel.

'...and the famous university, Brunel University, is named after him. And now we come...'

I looked around me. We were climbing a hill and there was nothing visible but a high wall which I had never noticed before.

'We come to the famous, the famous Exeter Wall,' I said. 'This wall was built to keep out Napoleon and –'

'It doesn't look that old,' said the Dutch or Belgian from before.

'Not that Napoleon,' I said. 'A different one. And it was this wall which inspired the –'

My mind was desperate to say 'the Great Wall of China'.

'The Great Wall of San Francisco,' I said desperately, 'which was utterly destroyed in the fire of 18, of 1876. Over to your left,' I added quickly, and forty heads out of forty-two turned, 'is the famous inn where, where Sir Francis Drake met Sir Walter Raleigh in 1588 after the battle of, after the Armada.'

Forty people looked at the inn, which was a dull pub with pebble-dashed walls and a homeless man singing outside it.

'Originally called the Dog and Dragon, the pub underwent many name changes until the twentieth century, when it settled on its present name of –'

I peered at the pub sign. It was worn and illegible. Still, if I couldn't read it, nor could anyone else.

'The Three Degrees,' I said wildly.

At that moment, a signal seemed to pass between the two men who had been following me. They moved forward down the bus and squeezed onto the end of a row of seats. One of them had his hand in his jacket again. I decided he was unlikely to execute me in front of forty tourists and ploughed on.

'To your right,' I said, then looked round and was delighted to see something I recognised, 'is a very famous hotel, the Telstar.'

Everyone turned to look at the Telstar Hotel.

'This hotel is the very hotel that the famous Telstar satellite is named after,' I said. Several eyebrows rose.

A hand went up.

'Questions afterwards,' I said firmly. But it was the same man again.

'What is that church over there?' he said, indicating a building whose spire I could just see in the distance.

'That?' I said. I had no idea. The problem with cathedral towns is that no other religious buildings get a look–in. In pop terms, cathedrals are the lead singers and all the other churches and chapels are bass players and drummers.

'Yes,' said my interrogator. 'What is it called?'

'Ah,' I said. 'That is a very important church indeed. Its name...'

I was drawing a mental blank. Eighty Dutch or Belgian eyes stared at me. For some reason I was feeling insulted that they didn't trust me.

'That,' I said suddenly, 'is the church of, the church of Saint God.'

'Saint God?' said the man. 'But God is not a saint.'

'Of course he's a saint,' I said. 'He's God. He's the chief saint. He's the boss of saints. And over there is Exeter Cathedral,' I added in some relief as somehow we found ourselves nearing the close. 'One of the oldest major cathedrals in Europe, with parts dating from, from the twelfth century and other, earlier centuries. It has –'

I was flagging now, and there was muttering among the Dutch or Belgians.

'It has,' I suddenly remembered, 'the oldest flying buttresses in England.'

'Flying buttresses?' said the man.

'Yes,' I said. 'Those bits outside, holding it up. That's what they're called. Flying buttresses.'

This piece of genuine if ordinary ecclesiastical knowledge seemed to impress my audience. As one, they nodded. And then to my relief, the bus slowed to a halt outside a large Tudor building whose existence I had never noticed before.

'And that concludes our tour,' I said. 'I hope you will enjoy the rest of your time in Devon.'

Like anyone who has been winging it, I was mildly drunk on my own flukish success. I should have stopped there. But instead I went on, 'And do not hesitate to ask me or the driver if you have any further queries.'

A hand went up. It belonged to one of the men and it was holding not a gun but a rolled-up newspaper. He said, loudly and clearly, 'I have a question.'

I may have swallowed. It may have been audible.

'I didn't mean that kind of question,' I said.

'Oh come,' he said, 'it won't take a moment.'

I looked around me. The tourists were craning their necks, eager to hear.

'Can you tell me please,' said the man. 'What is the Rawley Vulcan?'

I stared at him.

'I'm sorry,' I said. 'I don't know what you're talking about.'

'Are you sure?' he said, holding up his newspaper. 'I have a photograph of it right here.'

'You have a whole article,' I said. 'I'm certain there's nothing I can tell you that's not in the paper.'

The tourists were getting a bit restless. Their tour was over and there must be lots of other things in Exeter for them to be getting on with. And then one of them, the one I was beginning to think of as my friend, put his hand up and said, 'I think you are not the only one with questions, sir.'

The man with the magazine said, 'I'm sorry. You are right, other people need to speak to our excellent guide. Perhaps we can speak later, when everyone has dispersed.'

'Always here to help,' I said and to my immense relief the two men went down the stairs, presumably to lurk nearby with blackjacks.

'Now,' I said. 'Who else has questions about this lovely old city?'

Forty hands went up.

Finally we were done, and one by one the tourists filed off the bus and into whatever the rest of the day held for them. I lingered a while, pretending to dust my peaked cap, and trying to cram my tips – a sweaty, if sincere, collection of pound coins, Euros and dollars – into my pocket. Finally I could linger no more, and – feeling like a kid who was hanging round after school in the hope that the bullies had got bored and gone home – I made my way down the stairs into the street. I was absolutely terrified. And there they were, standing by a pillar box. One of them even waved at me while the other pretended to read the Rawley Vulcan article.

I wondered what to do next. The bus was pulling away, so I couldn't go and hide on that. The tourists had long evaporated in the direction of something called a Bake'N'Take. And running didn't seem like a good idea, because the two men looked violent in a pub sort of way. So, empty of ideas, and also very frightened, I just stood there. The two men stared at me for a moment. I stared back. The road was clear, and the two of them started to cross, with expectant grins on their faces.

And then, just as the first man, the one who had been waving at me, was about to step onto the pavement, a large old car appeared from nowhere and knocked him flying. I think I heard something in him crunch.

The nearside back door of the car opened. In the back seat, wrapped up in something that I was pretty sure was fur, was a very old woman.

'Get in,' she said.

I got in. Any port in a storm. Besides, the two men were recovering themselves now.

'Who are you?' I said to the old woman.

'Cora Vanstone,' she replied. 'Drive!' she shouted in a surprisingly loud voice to someone in the front, and the large, old car positively bolted away from the curve.

'Brandy?' said Cora Vanstone, as we headed out of the city. 'You look like you could do with some.'

CHAPTER FOUR

'A really good forgery presented at the right time and in suitable sur-
roundings will always appear above suspicion.'

   – AJB Kiddell, *Fakes and Reproductions in China, Glass and Other
Works of Art*

The Rolls-Royce – I couldn't tell you which kind it was, but it made
the Jag look like something from the future – was virtually racing
through the streets, which was good as it couldn't have been easier to
follow if it had had a giant fluorescent jelly on its roof and a sign that
read FOLLOW THE GIANT FLUORESCENT JELLY.

I drained my brandy.

'Thank you,' I said to Cora Vanstone.

She ignored me, which made sense. Upper–class people, of whom
I was sure Cora Vanstone was one, don't really have manners. By
which I don't mean they're actually rude, although they often are, but
rather that they don't need manners; they employ people to do things
for them, and have others specially bred, as it were, to look after their
estates, so they don't need politeness and manners to grease the wheels
of everyday existence. That's my theory anyway.

I took a good look at Cora. She was old, as I said, and bird-like, but
you'd have to say that whatever bird she was like wasn't one you'd
want to mess with, like a sparrow that knew martial arts, or a particularly hard wren. Nevertheless I felt safe with her, which was a bit
weird, given that she was a little old lady in the back of a vintage car.

'You're probably wondering what you're doing here,' she said.

'Yes,' I replied. 'It does seem rather odd.' I always find that when
I'm talking to people higher up the poshness ladder than me, I unconsciously start talking like them. In my head I sounded like I was doing
a commentary on the coronation.

If Cora Vanstone noticed my strangled RP tones, she didn't say.
Instead she stared at me with her cold blue porcelain eyes and said, 'It's
very simple. Hodge and I have been following you.'

I presumed that Hodge was her driver. I hoped so, anyway.

'I can't believe I didn't notice your car,' I said.

'Very amusing,' she said, although I wasn't joking. 'Hodge followed you on foot after he saw you with that fool Armstrong. He has military training, you know.'

I was still none the wiser, less so in fact. 'So…' I said, virtually miming knowledge.

'We had received information,' said Cora impatiently, 'that Mister Armstrong was on his way to Exeter. Apparently he had read some silly newspaper story for which he thought I was responsible and in a panic decided to rush down to Devon to, I don't know, sort things out. The man really is a fool.'

I didn't disagree with this, partly because I was still somewhat confused. And Cora Vanstone was still talking.

'I slightly regret writing to that man,' she said. 'He was most unhelpful when I telephoned him to see if he had received my letter. And he has been quite unpleasant since then.'

'He didn't tell me he'd spoken to you,' I said. I looked out of the window. We were now leaving the city and heading towards a large bypass.

'That doesn't surprise me,' she said. 'He never even mentioned to me that he was sending a subordinate to visit me.'

'I'm not exactly a subordinate,' I said. 'I'm more of a freelance –'

'I know what you are,' she said, sharply. 'Hodge looked you up on the internet. You sound like a bit of a fraud to me.'

This did strike me as rude, but I said nothing. After all, she had rescued me.

'I have my own methods,' I said, trying to sound more professional than I felt.

'I have no doubt,' she said. 'And I must admit I am intrigued. From what Hodge tells me, you have had some success where others have failed.'

'I suppose so,' I said, relieved that I had finally met someone who wasn't going to go on about the Rawley Vulcan all day.

'Pull in here,' said Cora Vanstone suddenly, and the Rolls-Royce turned off the road into a large car park.

'Where are we going?' I said as Hodge inched the car towards a small line of stationary vehicles.

'McDonald's,' said Cora. 'Hodge and I have missed our lunch and I'm starving.'

We sat in the car park, in the back of the Rolls-Royce, eating our McDonald's. I had a quarter pounder with cheese, Cora Vanstone had a Filet-O-Fish (she ate like a bird, too) and Hodge had a Happy Meal ('He collects the toys for his grandchildren,' explained Cora).

Hodge came round to the back of the car and collected our rubbish. I tried to catch his eye, but he just avoided my glance, not rudely but the way the guards do outside Buckingham Palace. As I watched his shaved neck head towards the car park waste bins, Cora Vanstone said, 'And do you suppose you will be able to tell me what my manuscript is?'

'I don't know,' I said, honestly enough. 'I haven't seen it, even as an image, so at the moment I have no idea what it's like.'

She nodded. 'Very well,' she said. 'I imagine therefore that you cannot tell me if the document is of interest.'

'It's definitely of interest,' I said. 'Unless it's the worst kind of forgery – like if it was done on a computer or the paper used is clearly very recent – it will be of interest. There's an odd duality, you see.'

'I do hope you're not talking nonsense to me,' said Cora Vanstone.

'I don't think I am,' I said. 'Because your document is very unusual. Most of the items I'm called up to investigate fall very clearly into one of two categories –'

'They're fake or they're not fake,' snapped Cora.

'Exactly,' I said. 'Although we prefer the term "not right".'

'And I prefer the term "fake".'

'Fair enough. But your document is intriguing because if it isn't not right, if it isn't fake, then it still falls into two categories. It's either by Daisy Ashford or it's by JM Barrie. If it's by Daisy, that's interesting, it's of value historically and financially; but if it's by Barrie, then it's of great value. Much greater value.'

'You know,' said Cora. 'I saw *Peter Pan* as a child.'

For a moment I thought she meant this sentence literally.

'The film?' I said.

'The play,' she said. 'Dreadful. Some silly woman years too old to play a boy, wobbling about on wires and going on endlessly about death and fairies. I've never seen the appeal myself.'

I didn't disagree with her, largely because I'd only ever seen the film, which in my memory is about ten minutes long and features one of the most dislikable central characters of all time.

'The thing is,' she said. 'I actually hope the manuscript is by Daisy Ashford. I've never liked this mania for uncovering secrets. People seem to love crowing over unpleasant discoveries. As though they're looking for proof that the world is crooked and unfair.'

'The world is crooked and unfair,' I said.

'I do know that, Mister Bread,' said Cora Vanstone. 'Hodge, let's go home. It's time we got this nonsense over with.'

The Rolls-Royce glided out of the car park and onto the bypass but when it came to the exit for Budleigh Salterton, it carried on.

'Isn't that our turning?' I said.

'Oh, we're not going to my house,' said Cora Vanstone. 'That wouldn't do at all. Not with the kind of people that you seem to attract.'

'Where are we going then? Kentucky Fried Chicken?' I managed not to add.

'Somewhere public,' she said. Then Cora Vanstone smiled at me, an act so surprising that I almost recoiled in shock.

'Do you like shells, Mister Bread?' she said.

After a few miles of passing places which seemed almost wilfully to start with 'Ex', the Rolls-Royce drove through Exton and turned off the main road towards Exmouth and made its way down a country lane that seemed to have got lost. As the car turned a corner, I could see a small house. It was entirely round, with a bit stuck on the top like an afterthought. The Rolls drove nearer and parked a few metres away.

'I love to come here,' said Cora Vanstone. 'It's one of my favourite places.'

'A La Ronde,' I said, some vague memory of a television programme about unusual locations surfacing at last.

'The Parminters,' she said, nodding. 'They had the whole thing
built, and they lived there, two spinster ladies. And their shells.'

Hodge opened a door and helped Cora out onto the grass. He left
me to fend for myself.

'You are familiar with Italy?' said Cora.

'A little,' I said.

'The exterior is based on the Basilica of San Vitale at Ravenna,' she
said. 'And of course the shells are Italian.'

'Of course,' I said. I'd forgotten about the shells.

We made our way slowly up to the house while I trawled my
memory. A La Ronde – in reality a sixteen-sided house – was a
dinky curiosity, home to Jane and Mary Parminter, two cousins who
retreated from the world in the late eighteenth century to a house that
they decorated, not with tapestries and vases, but seashells. The effect
was said to be delightful, if you liked that sort of thing. Cora Vanstone
clearly did.

'It's closed,' I said.

'Not to me,' she said, as Hodge produced a large key and opened
the front door.

We entered and I was immediately struck by what I presumed was
the odour of a lot of old shells. This effect was not improved by the
smallness of the house. Clearly the Parminter cousins were not giants.
From somewhere, Hodge produced a couple of folding chairs, and
then opened a small cupboard, from which he took a briefcase. He
brought it out and gave it to Cora Vanstone.

'The moment of truth, Mister Bread,' she said. 'Are you ready?'

I wanted to say that I was not, and that the smell of old seashells was
getting to me somewhat, and could we do this somewhere else. But
none of these seemed like particularly convincing reasons, and besides
I wasn't going to conduct a forensic test, I was just going to cast an
eye over some old notebooks. But still, I had some backside-covering
to do before we got started.

'I feel I should say in advance,' I said, 'that any comments I make
here are preliminary and not in any way binding on Pring's.'

'Of course,' Cora Vanstone said, a little impatiently. 'We realise that you do not have the authority to act for anyone, much less make any decisions.'

I felt this was a little harsh, but at least it got me off the hook if I was wrong.

'All right then,' I said and held my hands out for the briefcase. Instead, Cora opened it herself with a click, the lid facing me so I was unable to see the contents, and appeared to be riffling through whatever was inside before finally coming to a decision and handing me a single piece of paper.

I looked at the paper before reading what, if anything, was written on it.

'This sheet has been ripped from a notebook or journal,' I said. 'Quite recently, too. Did you do this?'

Time passed. I suspected from the silence that I had not asked a suitable question. Hodge coughed. And then Cora Vanstone sighed, a sigh thinner than a cucumber sandwich with the crust cut off.

'I really don't feel we can talk freely here,' she said. 'Hodge, can you escort us to the Shell Gallery?'

My first reaction to this remark was, I only mentioned the paper was torn. My second was, oh great, more shells. The Shell Gallery – located in the stuck-on bit of the house – was up a flight of stairs, where Hodge was carefully leading Cora. It was a slender rim of a gallery, punctuated with windows shaped like diamonds and festooned with the mortal remains of a lot of shelled animals. I had to admit that it was quite beautiful. Cora leaned on a railing that seemed barely fit for purpose, while Hodge clutched the case to his chest.

'Are you sure you wouldn't be more comfortable sitting down?' I said.

'Naturally I would be,' she replied. 'But we are not here for our comfort, are we?'

'Why have we come upstairs, may I ask?' I said.

'The windows offer added… visibility,' said Cora Vanstone. And she was right. I could see over several fields and as far as a small, odd-looking chapel.

'The Point-in-View Chapel,' said Cora. 'Also built by the Parminters. It is named after its own motto.'

She looked me in the eye. 'Some point in view,' she said, 'we all pursue.'

I felt I had to say something so I said, 'How true,' and wished I hadn't because it rhymed and made me feel silly. Instead I looked at Hodge, who was clearly scanning the horizon. For what, I didn't know. If Cora Vanstone felt uneasy, she didn't look it. She seemed to be almost chatty.

'You see those oaks?' she said.

I nodded. I can barely tell the difference between an oak tree and a Christmas tree, but I didn't want to have trees explained to me as well as everything else.

'They were planted at the insistence of Miss Jane Parminter,' said Cora Vanstone. 'In her will she made two requests: one, that she be interred in the chapel in an upright coffin and two, that the grove of oak trees you see now – and I quote from memory – "shall remain standing, and the hand of man shall not be raised up against them till Israel returns and is restored to the Land of Promise".'

'I beg your pardon?' I said.

'The oaks,' she said. 'They must never be taken down "till Israel returns and is restored to the Land of Promise".'

'But hasn't Israel –' I began.

'Not that Israel,' she said. 'The one in the Bible.'

'I thought Israel was the one in the Bible,' I said, and received for my pains a very severe glare.

'She wanted the Jews to use the oak to build ships, you see,' said Cora Vanstone. 'To return to Israel.'

I was now entirely speechless.

'Imagine that, Mister Bread,' she said. 'Imagine being so far sighted, and so dedicated to an ideal. I wish in this modern world we could be filled with such altruism.'

Hodge was looking a bit antsy, and I couldn't blame him. We'd been up here talking about trees and Israel for long enough. Cora Vanstone appeared to agree because she now said: 'You asked me if I was responsible for tearing this paper out. And I –'

There was a noise outside, like a car's wheels on gravel. Hodge turned and ran down the narrow stairs.

'Give me the piece of paper,' said Cora Vanstone, in a sharp tone.

'It'll be fine with me,' I said. 'What's happening outside?'

And then there was a loud bang and one of the diamond windows exploded. Cora exclaimed as the glass turned into powder millimetres from her eyes.

I was transfixed. The noise and the shock had paralysed me. Was someone *shooting* at us? I unfroze again and turned to ask Cora if she was all right, but she was heading for the stairs. Clearly the right decision, I thought, and followed her.

It's hard trying to run away from a possible assailant when you're trying to get down a staircase and the person in front of you is frail and slow. Fortunately Hodge reappeared and, without a word, ran up the stairs. Pausing only to give her an apologetic look, he picked Cora Vanstone up bodily and headed for a side door I hadn't seen, kicking it open and heading outside before I could even reach the bottom of the stairs.

By now I was surrounded by what felt like a storm of bullets. The things were raining down from all directions, and I covered my head and cowered on the floor as glass and shells rained down from the gallery like a mad sea harvest and ran across the floor. I was terrified and wanted more than anything else to run – but fear and a rare burst of common sense kept me where I was. Somehow I managed to wedge myself in behind a ridiculously small couchette. It wouldn't hide me from anyone who came inside the house, but it would keep me safe from casual gunmen, if there were such a thing.

And then the shooting stopped. My ears took a while to get used to the silence; my heart took a while to stop pounding. I wouldn't have been surprised if people going past on the road outside could have heard it: to me, it sounded like a gorilla trying to break down a steel door.

I was petrified, yes, but I was also furious. I was filled with a sense of ridiculous hurt and outrage at my situation. How dare someone shoot at me? I thought. I work for an auction house, not the mafia. And then: if you want to shoot someone, fuck off to London and shoot Armstrong. I was not thinking clearly, to say the least.

Then I thought I heard a car crunch off into the lane. I waited a full twenty minutes and then, when I was certain I was safe, came out from behind the couchette and looked around. Nothing but shells and plaster indicated that anyone had been here.

I opened the door cautiously and went outside. The Rolls-Royce stood on the lawn, its doors open. There were tyre marks on the grass, but no sign of the other vehicle, and no signs of a struggle. I walked over to the Rolls. There was no-one inside, and no briefcase either – I could only guess that that was the reason the unknown gunmen had come, and had taken the case and Hodge and Vanstone with them.

And then I noticed that the Rolls' engine was on and the keys were in the ignition. Hodge must have managed to start the car before he had been overpowered. I felt in my pocket. I still had the piece of paper Cora Vanstone had handed me.

I had a car. I had a piece of paper. Now all I needed was a plan.

'Oh, sod all this,' I said to the sixteen-sided building, 'I'm going to get an ice cream.'

The Rolls-Royce was reasonably easy to drive. Once I'd got used to the gears and the eerie quietness of the engine, it fairly purred along. The only problem was its visibility. Even in East Devon, where some of the population are not so much older than God, as they used to teach Him at primary school, a vintage car tended to stand out. And now that I was certain bad people were in the vicinity, with guns and malice, I really should have dumped the Rolls and walked into town.

But I really wanted an ice cream. And I wanted to eat it on the beach, in peace, watching the sun go down. So I drove to the seafront, parked at the furthest end, away from the camper vans and the boy racers, found a Mister Softee van and bought a 99 with alleged raspberry syrup. Then I sat on the beach with my back to the sea wall and watched the sun go down.

It was by far the best thing that had happened to me all week. The beach at Exmouth is long, and curves slowly round. The sky was enormous and went from blue and white to gold and red with a pleasing slowness, like there was no need for any hurry anywhere. Dog walkers dotted the beach and a few windsurfers taking advantage of the last light of the day crossed my sight line, but apart from that, I had the view to myself. The 99 was pretty good as well, the slightly metallic taste of the ice cream taking me back to my additive-crammed childhood. After forty minutes or so, I was beginning to get cold, and in the fading light it was hard to see if the tide was coming in or not, so I got up, stretched a bit, and headed back to my parking space. Which no longer contained the Rolls-Royce.

I ducked behind a convenient camper van and looked around. But whoever had taken the Rolls was gone. They might have been looking for me, but I supposed I would have been hard to see, sitting against a wall in the evening shadow. Probably it was just the car they wanted. A small dusting of powdery glass suggested that they'd cut their way in through the window, although how they'd started the car was a mystery.

An old man with an almost older dog was staring at me.

'That your car, was it?' he said.

'Yes,' I said.

'Got towed,' he explained, gleeful like all witnesses.

'But I paid the parking.'

'Can't have,' he said. 'Else they wunt have towed it.'

'It's free after six,' I pointed out.

He shrugged.

'Wunt council towed it, anyway. Private tow.'

'What do you mean, private tow?'

'Red truck. Council truck's white. With green bits.'

I thanked him for his information and walked off.

After a desultory pint in an equally desultory pub, I decided now would be a good time to have a plan, before someone else attacked, punched, shot, dumped or just patronised me like a bastard toff. I needed a breathing space, somewhere I would – with luck – be safe for a moment from the insane pile-on that was currently my life.

I walked to the train station, which was a single platform hoarding a single track, and bought a ticket to Exeter. At least I could get back

in the Jag (assuming that hadn't been towed as well) and find somewhere to spend the night. I was well aware that I had the piece of
notebook paper in my pocket still but I didn't want to look at it until
I was settled in some form of comfort and away from any distractions,
like people trying to hunt me down and shoot me.

It wasn't much of a plan, I knew. On the other hand, I didn't have
anything else on that night.

The train – more of a bus on rails, really – arrived, and I got on.
Half an hour later, after an uneventful journey spent looking at the
mild beauty of the Exe estuary at night, I got off at Exeter St Davids
and went to find the Jag. Mercifully, it was still there, unmolested
by parking attendants, and nobody had broken into it, removed its
contents or rendered it undrivable. I sat in it, transferred the scrap of
paper to my wallet, turned the Jag's heater up and did a quick situation check. The satnav was working and my phone still had charge. I
could only hope my dad was still up.

I don't know why I hadn't thought of my dad earlier. I suppose it's
because he's only lived in Devon for a couple of years – although
thinking about it, it's probably more like five – or maybe it's because
he only moved here after he got divorced from my mum, and I'm
still coming to terms with that. Not their separation as such, just the
whole idea of a couple in their sixties who'd been married for decades
suddenly jacking in their marriage at a point in their lives when most
people are settling in for the long haul and the silver anniversary
and all that kind of thing. Or maybe I just didn't associate him with
Devon.

All of which went some way to explaining why I suddenly realised
I had no idea what his address was. This wasn't too surprising: I could
tell you right now the name, address, postcode and telephone number
of the house I grew up in, even though we moved from there when
I was fifteen. Same with the house my parents lived in for twenty-
five years after that. But when it came to Dad's new house – cottage,
rather, as he was at least interested in some of the trappings of the
retired – I couldn't even remember the name. I had a vague feeling it
might be 'Rosebud', but on reflection this seemed unlikely.

I did at least have his mobile number. My dad was surprisingly up to date when it came to technology, updating his iPod every few years so he could listen to his absurdly large collection of Italian operas ('My only rule is it has to be in foreign,' he told me. 'The words don't sound the same if you can understand them'), and upgrading his mobile phone whenever he thought the salesman might be laughing at him ('Bumfluff moustaches the lot of them,' he said, but he still upgraded the phones).

I called his number and the phone went to voicemail. This didn't surprise me: my dad lived in a small valley surrounded by big hills, and besides he kept turning his phone off whenever he 'wasn't using it'. To you and me, this might mean whenever we were asleep, but to my dad, it meant whenever he went to the bathroom, or was in the garden, or watching BBC Four documentaries about the First World War so he could call me up and complain about them (even though he was too young to remember the Second World War, let alone the first, and I hadn't made the documentaries, but that didn't seem to matter to my dad. He could complain about anything. I once saw him complain to my mum that she'd made his favourite meal and when she pointed out, sanely, that he'd actually asked her to make his favourite meal, he said, 'But you know I like a surprise every now and then.' The more I think about it, the less odd their divorce seems).

I left a message about being in the vicinity and wondered what I should do now. Dad could call in ten seconds time or he might not notice at all, having fallen asleep in front of *Trench Britannia* or some such with a bottle of Guinness and a cheese sandwich on the sofa next to him (despite being an ex-company director – light aircraft hire – Dad always drank and ate like a farm labourer in a 1930s documentary). Thinking of my dad's dining habits had the effect of actually making me hungry, so I got out of the Jag and went in search of food. I was keen to have a pint or similar, but I knew I'd be driving soon and, besides, I didn't want to turn up completely pissed at my dad's.

There was nothing open – at least, nothing I wanted. I passed a place that looked like a burger joint but sold heaps of red cabbage and shredded meat on breadboards, an Italian restaurant where every table was crammed with twelve–year–old girls all eating pizzas the size of Kent, and a chip shop where everything from the forks and the plates to, quite possibly, the fish and the chips seemed to be made of polystyrene. Finally, out of sheer despair, I decided to compromise. I would drive out of Exeter, head towards my dad's, and find some sort of country pub and have a proper dinner – without, I told myself, any beer. Well, maybe a half. Or a shandy. Or a lager top.

I got back in the Jag and drove off. After about twenty minutes, I had entirely failed to find somewhere I'd like to stop. Have you ever had that feeling where if you just keep going a little bit further, you'll find the perfect place to eat, or drink, or stay? I was in that mood as I passed pub after pub, until suddenly I realised that I was incredibly hungry and that I would have to abandon choice and pull in at the next place. And there it was. A sign proclaimed that it was formerly The Ship and Lion Inn, but it had recently changed hands and was now a proud new addition to the Three For One Inn family.

I sighed and drove into the car park. At least I wouldn't have to look at the menu, I reflected, as I walked up the path to the front door.

I went in and was immediately overwhelmed by a weird variant of déjà vu. Because while I'd never been in this pub before, it was laid out in exactly the same manner as the last Three For One Inn I'd gone to. I wasn't sure at all if this was company policy: after all, this was clearly a reasonably old building and surely the owners wouldn't have gone to all the trouble and expense of completely gutting the place to make it look like the other ones. Or would they?

I'd once been told by Roger Armstrong about one of our clients, a wealthy (obviously) Russian who'd flown over, or possibly even been flown over, to look at some agricultural paintings by eighteenth-century English artists – you know, those weird fat pig ones – that had come into our possession. Pring's had valued this man's custom so highly that they'd even found him a quaint – if high-end – hotel to stay in, figuring that if he was so into old stuff, then he'd love a half-timbered, wonky-staired, Queen-Bess-slept-here kind of place. Instead, our potential client took one look around the Tudor bar, stormed out and checked into a nearby Hilton so generic even the staff looked cloned. It turned out that the man travelled so much he needed the stale familiarity of hotels that were identical to one another because that way he knew where everything, including himself, was.

And perhaps it was the same way with the Three For One Inn chain. Maybe even now, as I sat on a bar stool identical to one I'd parked my backside on a few hours, or was it days, before, workmen were gutting pubs and filleting bars all around the country and replacing their innards with the same template interior. Perhaps there was even a kit you could buy, to turn your local into a fully authorised Three For One Inn.

I abandoned this train of thought, picked up a menu that I knew better than the Lord's Prayer, and looked for a member of staff. There wasn't one. I waited a minute or two. After the second minute, I was beginning to wonder if perhaps I shouldn't go into the kitchen myself and rustle something up, when a tall boy with the nostrils of a horse shuffled into sight.

'Sorry,' he said, in tones that suggested he was a stranger to regret. 'I was serving those gemmen.'

He nodded towards the other side of the bar. There, selecting their cutlery with intense concentration, were the two men from the white Prius.

'It's all right,' I said, 'I'm not hungry.'

I got up and was about to make my way towards the door when the boy said, 'Are you not with them, then?'

'Pardon?'

'They were just saying they were waiting for their friends. Are you not with them, then?'

This was ridiculous. Now I didn't know if I was being followed by dangerous killers or just a pair of nutters who wanted to split their dinner bill with me.

'No,' I said. 'I don't know them.'

'Only I seen your car and it fit the bill,' said the boy.

I had to work on this sentence for a moment until it made sense.

'When you drove up,' he went on. 'I was looking out the car park and I seen you drive up. I seen your car and it fit the bill.'

There was no way that one of the men wasn't going to look up at any second. I was torn between making a run for it or carrying on with this bizarre conversation. In the end, I couldn't help it. I said:

'What do you mean, my car fit the bill?'

'They were saying how the man they were meeting had a very nice car,' said the boy. 'Like a special one. So when I seen your car –'

'It fit the bill,' I said. 'I see. Look, great, I have to go now.'

I bolted for the door. I heard one of the white Prius men call the boy over and prayed they hadn't seen me. I made it to the Inn's porch and was about to hurry into the car park when, with a massive wallop, the door opened and whacked me on the forehead. I staggered backwards, stunned for a moment. An actual red mist filled my vision, one so vividly red that for a moment I thought my eyes were filling with blood.

This time I really had had enough. I couldn't even go for a drink without being almost killed by some moron who opened doors without checking anyone was behind them. I decided then and there that I was going to demand an apology and if I didn't get one, I was going to knock his head off – perhaps literally.

And I was half a second away from doing it, too, when I saw him. Or his Barbour jacket and stupid tweedy hat, anyway. It was the oik with the sports car. The one who'd filmed himself overtaking. Greg. Penelope's love interest. And he was being hailed – waved at – by the two men at the bar.

He wasn't alone, either. He was with a woman. A dead woman. Lily George.

I turned on my heel, walked back into the pub, and left through a back door.

Once in the car again, I found that I couldn't stop shaking. I was really spooked. Actually, 'spooked' didn't even begin to cover it. 'Terrified and confused' was probably more like it. 'Bricking it' was in there too. I felt like one of those Ancient Greeks who were always being persecuted by the gods for completely random reasons, like everyone on Mount Olympus was bored and felt like mucking about with some mortals. This was, I realised, unlikely, but then everything that had happened to me in the last few days had been an unusual combination of unlikely, random and relentless, like a stream of coincidences involving psychotic killer steamrollers.

I tried to calm down. I saw a lay-by coming up, the kind truckers pull up in when they want a kip, and I drove into it. I turned the engine off and tried to think. It wasn't easy, as my mind appeared to have become a kind of factory devoted to manufacturing panic and nonsense. What was Greg doing there? Was he looking for Penelope? But Penelope wasn't with me. She'd left me at Exeter. Maybe he didn't know that. How would he even know she was with me anyway? Was the Jag bugged? And what about the two men from the white Prius? Did he know them? Did they know him? Then there was Cora Vanstone and the shooting incident. Were they behind that too? Was Greg? He looked the kind of oaf who would be good at firing guns. But they did too.

And what about Lily? She was dead, it said so in the paper. How could she be here if she was dead? I did some deep breathing, realising I wasn't making any sense, even to myself. If she was in the pub, she couldn't be dead. If she wasn't dead – I had no idea. No thoughts were coming. I realised my brain was pretty much running on empty and decided to just stop thinking for a minute. I closed my eyes and did some deep breathing. After a few seconds of this, I became quite dizzy and there was an egg coming up on my forehead which was beginning to throb purposefully, so I stopped. I felt a vibrating in my pocket and took my phone out. What with one thing and another, I had quite forgotten to check it for messages. Now I noticed there was one, on voicemail.

'Bloody thing,' said my dad's voice. 'Keeps you waiting ten minutes with a load of cobblers about if you want to change your message and then just when you've given up it goes beep and – anyway, I'm home now, and I'm going to be up for a while because that feller's on, you know, you don't think he's funny but I quite like him, and –'

The phone beeped and my dad's message ended. I turned on the satnav and reckoned I could be at his within the hour. I hoped he had some food in: I was starving.

'There was a recent concert at Maison Albert by the Mothers of Invention, who are one of the most controversial groups around, I suppose…'

This one's definitely not a Festive Fifty. Peel is hosting an edition of the radio show *Top Gear* – co-hosting it, in fact, with another DJ called Pete Drummond. It's October 1967, so both Peel and Drummond have only been BBC disc jockeys for a few months. Their banter is jocular but slightly forced, and Peel sounds odd, a mixture of slightly fruity (his pronunciation of 'groups' is almost ringmasterish) and slightly twee. It's also odd to hear records by Pink Floyd (sorry, *The* Pink Floyd) and The Velvet Underground being played for the first time.

This tape is a favourite. Normally I don't play tapes twice, but I've loved this particular show ever since I found it in MP3 form on the internet and, now that I've transferred it onto cassette, I've discovered that it's a very good accompaniment to night-driving. It's a shorter show than most, and it's recorded in late–night mono, with static occasionally blowing in, but maybe that's part of the appeal. It's a message from a lost world.

'Have you ever heard of Simon and Garfunkel?' jokes Drummond, and Peel replies, *'By Jove, that does ring a bell! And it's an awfully clever way of getting into the next record. You'll notice if you're particularly perceptive that in the middle of this record there is a spoken bit in which they mention Mister Leitch, and of course Mister Leitch is Donovan. This is called Fakin' It.'*

I nearly stopped the car. I'd heard that song before. 'Fakin' It'. Not one of Simon and Garfunkel's best-known songs at all, but it had been a single. I knew this because my dad owned it. And I knew my dad had it because he kept talking about it. He'd play it on his somehow annoying 1970s hi-fi system with its glowing valves and then he'd take it off and show the label to whichever of my teenage friends had unwittingly expressed an interest in it.

'See that?' he'd say as I cringed both inwardly and outwardly as they peered at the label, trying to work out whatever the hell he was on about. After a few seconds, my dad would take their baffled silence as a cue to carry on and say, 'Look at the timing. 2.74. That means two minutes and seventy-four seconds.'

Most of my friends didn't react to this. Some of them would get it though.

'That's right,' my dad would say as I looked around for any friendly earth that might want to swallow me up. 'Two minutes seventy-four seconds. And there's only sixty seconds in a minute. You see,' he would say, almost lighting an imaginary pipe in my mind, 'the song was really three minutes and fourteen seconds long, but in those days the radio wouldn't play a song that was longer than three minutes, so Paul Simon changed the label to read 2.74.'

This announcement was rarely met with enthusiasm. Once he tried the 2.74 routine out on one of my girlfriends and, after she had dumped me at school the next day, I hid the record in the coalshed. For all I know it may still be there, waiting for the dads of tomorrow to annoy future teenagers.

As Simon and Garfunkel's muffled guitars play out in the dashboard-lit darkness of the Jag, down the road I can see what the satnav tells me I should be seeing: the yellow lights of my dad's cottage. I fade down the music and turn into Dad's driveway. I turn the engine off, get my stuff from the Jag and walk up to Dad's front door.

I don't ring the bell, but knock quietly. I know Dad will be watching TV with the sound down low, waiting for me. Sure enough, a few moments later, the door opens, and there he is. Looking a few years older, wearing a cardigan my mum would have burned on sight, but looking well.

'Hello, Robert,' my dad says. 'Come in and have a cup of tea.'

Part Two

Are you lost Daddy I arsked tenderly.
Shut up he explained.
  – Ring Lardner, *The Young Immigrunts*

CHAPTER FIVE

'I could not know what it was like to be dead. But I could know what it would be like to be thought to be dead, which I engineered.'

– Robert Lenkiewicz

'Don't call me that,' I said. 'Hello, Dad.'

I stepped into the cottage and his warm but awkward hug. My dad always hugged me like he was a huge marionette with stiff wooden arms. I kind of liked it, but it still took some getting used to and I was glad he only ever did it when nobody else was around.

'Why not?' said my dad. 'It's your name. Your mother and I chose it. Oh well,' he added, closing the door, 'your loss... "Charlie".'

I decided not to make a thing of it. 'Is there a cup of tea going?' I said, as he took my bag. My dad was very big on taking people's bags, but never seemed to have a clear idea of what to do with them. He could never decide whether he should take the bag into another room, perhaps one upstairs, and get it out of the way, or just set it down in the hall until it was needed, and as a consequence would end up holding it at some bizarre, indecisive angle for seemingly ever. With this particular bag, which frankly a baby could have carried, he had settled for holding it just under his chin like a weird bulgy violin.

I put him out of his misery, took the bag off him and went into what I presumed was the sitting room. There I was met by a bizarre collection of flower-patterned armchairs and sofas and a fireplace big enough to render a ballroom muggy.

'The settees and so on came with the cottage,' explained my dad, seeing my reaction, 'and I know the fireplace is a bit big, but once you've got the fire going, it goes on for ever.'

And to be fair, my dad had got a regular inferno going. I noticed his own favourite chair – a dog-ridden thing he'd had since he got married – was shoved as far back from the fireplace as possible. I sat down on some sort of antique milking stool and tried to warm my hands without actually setting them alight.

Dad brought in a tea tray laden with cups that were somehow even more floral than the furniture.

'Came with the cottage as well,' he said.

'Where's all your stuff, Dad?' I asked.

'Storage,' he replied. I didn't ask why he didn't get his own stuff out of storage and replace everything. I wasn't sure the answer would make me happy.

'So,' said my dad, sipping from a cup that a hamster in a frock would have found too chintzy, 'what brings you down this way?'

'I'll tell you later,' I was about to say, when suddenly a wave of weariness overcame me. Weariness with the whole ridiculousness of the past few days and with having, I suppose, to put up with Armstrong and Cora Vanstone and even Penelope and her appearances and disappearances. Also, yes, being possibly hunted down by armed men. So instead of doing what I would normally have done with my dad, which is tell him a severely edited version of events, I told him the lot. From being hired by Armstrong to check out the possible JM Barrie document and meeting Penelope all the way to the visit to A La Ronde and the constant reappearance of the two men in the white Prius. I left out the Rawley Vulcan, of course, because nobody wants their dad thinking ill of them, and I didn't mention Cora Vanstone's name because of some vague commitment to client confidentiality, but all in all, it was probably the most honest recounting of anything I'd done in the last ten years. Fifteen, maybe.

My dad listened without comment to the whole story, pausing only to sip his tea with a sound like a lion ripping the side of a tent using its teeth. When I'd finished, he didn't say a word for a few seconds. Then he got up, opened a completely fake-looking sixteenth–century–style wooden globe and took out a bottle of malt whisky and two tumblers. He poured two whiskies and set them both down on a low table in front of us.

'I see,' he said, and drank some whisky. I did the same. I knew he was thinking, because he'd unconsciously closed one eye. For some reason my dad could only think with one eye shut, like he was some kind of darts player of the mind.

Then he said, 'Of course, you know all about JM Barrie being a forger.'

'Pardon?' I said.

'JM Barrie,' said my dad. 'He was a forger. It's a well-known fact.' And he leaned back, virtually puffing with satisfaction on an imaginary briar.

I was transported back thirty years via the magic of irritation. I tried to sound calm as I said, 'What do you mean, JM Barrie was a forger?'

My dad, enjoying the effect he was having on me a bit too much for my liking, decided not to milk the moment any longer.

'I read it somewhere,' he said. 'Hang on.'

And he went off towards a bookshelf, leaving me to ball my fists in a curiously nostalgic way.

'Here it is,' he said, returning with a book. 'It's a biography of JM Barrie.'

'Why have you got a biography of JM Barrie?' I said.

'Came with the cottage,' said my dad. 'I had a flick through a couple of months ago when there was nothing on the telly. Very interesting man.'

He opened the book at the back, presumably looking for an index, turned to a page in the middle and handed me the book.

'Here,' he said. I reached for the book but my dad wasn't done yet.

'You see, JM Barrie was in love with this woman, Sylvia Du Maurier,' he said. 'She was married, though, and had five boys, who are the basis for the Lost Boys in *Peter Pan*. And one of them was called Peter, so you can see he was quite close to the family.'

'I see,' I said, resolving to read the book for myself when he'd gone to bed.

'Anyway, Sylvia – her father was Gerald Du Maurier, who was a famous writer, and her niece was Daphne Du Maurier, who wrote *The Birds*,' said my dad, who seemed to have turned into a kind of music–hall memory man, 'Sylvia wrote her will, in which she said – here it is...'

My dad put on his reading glasses.

'"What I would like,"' he read, '"would be if Jimmy would come to Mary & that the two together would be looking after the boys & the house." "Jimmy" being JM Barrie, you see.'

'Yes,' I said, wondering if he'd be offended if I leapt up and grabbed the book from his hands, 'it's very clear.'

'Ah, but that's where you're wrong,' said my dad, and at that moment only filial affection prevented me from bundling him into a cupboard and nailing it shut. 'Because someone looked at the original will and it didn't say "Jimmy" at all. It said "Jenny", who was the sister of that Mary she mentions. It only said "Jimmy" in a copy of the will that Barrie had written out himself.'

My dad peered at me triumphantly over his glasses.

'Barrie wrote himself into the will so he'd get custody of her children,' he said. 'He forged the will.'

I stared at him. 'Can I see that?' I said. My dad handed the book over and I scanned the page. He was right. The author of the book did concede that Barrie may have made a simple copying error, but it was hard to see how you might mistake someone else's name for your own. Whether intentionally or not – and I was going with intentionally – JM Barrie had altered a very important document.

'So if he faked that...' said my dad, thoughtfully letting me reach my own conclusion.

'Then he could have faked the Daisy Ashford book,' I said.

'Exactly,' said my dad.

I looked at the book. It was all very clear. There was some stuff about Barrie's relationship with the children which I didn't like the look of but the central fact remained: Barrie was a forger.

'Churchill suspected him,' said my dad.

'Churchill?' I said, confused by this sudden change of tack.

'Winston Churchill,' said my dad, in case I thought he was talking about Derek or Jennifer Churchill. 'He reckoned he'd written *The Young Visiters.*'

'Really?' I said. 'How do you know that?'

'I read a lot,' said my dad. 'More than you do, by the sound of it.'

I ignored this remark.

'You used to read a lot,' continued my dad, 'when you were Robert.'

He sounded tired. I decided to call a halt to this.

'I need my bed,' I said. 'Let's have a chat in the morning, shall we?'

'All right,' said my dad.

He stood up. I stood up.

'Thanks for telling me about the will,' I said.

'No problem,' said my dad. 'See you tomorrow, son.'

There was another hug, this time slightly less warm, and we went our separate ways.

One of the things about staying with a parent when they've moved out of the house you grew up in is that you never really feel that you're home. Of course, in one major way you're not home because you're an adult and you have your own home. But there's still the lingering fact that wherever your parents live is always your home. Generally you're welcome there, there are people and items which you associate with your childhood, and even if it isn't the place where you grew up, then it's at least an echo of that place.

Dad's cottage was no exception. I may not have been in my old room, full of the posters and toys of my youth, but the spare room in the cottage was a kind of store room for our shared past. On a small shelf were my old books. On the dressing table was a random collection of toys from my infancy – a stuffed rat, a broken Thunderbirds rocket, that sort of thing. And at the foot of the bed was a small cardboard box, the kind you might post something in.

I pulled it out. I was tired, but curiosity is like adrenaline. I found a pair of nail scissors, slit open the box – it had been taped shut and clearly never opened since it had been posted – and lifted the lid.

I could hear the toilet flush outside.

'Dad,' I called.

My dad came in, clearly keen to end the evening on a less awkward note.

'What is it?' he said.

I showed him the box. It was full of cassette tapes.

'Oh,' he said. 'It came in the post. About a year ago. It's addressed to you.'

'Why didn't you tell me about it?'

'I thought I'd give it you when you came down. And now I have. What's A and A?'

'That's who forwarded it.'

'I got that. I meant who are –'

'I don't even remember buying this. But thanks for looking after it.'

'Any time,' said my dad. 'Anyway, good night.'

My dad closed the door behind him. I looked at the tapes again. There must have been forty of them, mostly in their original boxes but, infuriatingly, all unmarked. Whoever had originally recorded the tapes had clearly never got round to labelling any of them. There was no note from the seller, no helpful list of contents or indeed the slightest indication of what they were. And I had no memory of buying them.

I was now so tired I could no longer think. 'Nice one, Charlie,' I said to myself and put the box in my bag to examine later. I turned out the light, tried to ignore the sounds of bats and cows outside, and fell asleep.

I awoke the next morning to the sound of banging and crashing. At first I thought the cottage was being demolished but I quickly realised this was unlikely and looked at my watch. 7.30, my dad's favourite time to get up, which meant he was probably having a shower. A faint whoosh from the next room confirmed this, so I decided that the horrendous racket was probably the boiler, as for some reason nobody who lives in the country ever has a normal water–heating system. This one was no exception, sounding as it did like a huge robot being smashed to pieces with its own arms.

I put on some clothes and went downstairs to make myself some breakfast. I went into the kitchen and was confronted with an Aga. I think Agas are among the most annoying inventions of all time. They're very good for heating rooms, but then so are fan heaters, and fan heaters don't take hours to get going, weigh six tons or have hundreds of pointless warm compartments where nothing can actually be cooked. I could see a sort of circle thing which was probably good for putting frying pans on, but I only wanted some toast. There was no toaster, so in the end I lay some slices of bread on the circle thing until they got a bit hard around the edges and managed with that. There was the obligatory unlabelled jar of something jam–like in a cupboard and a butter dish which, despite its proximity to the Aga, contained a hard, unyielding slab of what could just as easily have been cheese or soap as butter.

I found a kettle and a jar of instant coffee and made the kind of breakfast a soldier in the trenches would have found unsatisfying.

From upstairs came the sound of an aircraft carrier being throttled, which presumably meant that my dad had finished his shower. Sure enough, a few minutes later he appeared in the kitchen, fully dressed and shaved.

'So what are your plans for today?' he said, pulling out a grill from inside the Aga that I hadn't seen and layering it with slices of bread.

'I don't know,' I said. 'I suppose I should head back to London.'

'What about the job you're on? Seeing the manuscript and that?'

'There's not much point, really. I don't imagine after what's happened I'll be seeing Cora Vanstone again and I very much doubt she'll be wanting to see me –'

I stopped. My dad was giving me a very odd look. I realised he was confused. Of course, I hadn't mentioned Cora last night and he was probably wondering what I was on about.

'Cora Vanstone?' he said, confirming my hypothesis.

'Yes,' I said, 'she's the woman I told you about. The one who took me to A La Ronde. I was supposed to go to her house – she lives at East Budleigh.'

'I know where Cora Vanstone lives,' said my dad. 'I play bowls with her.'

A powerful silence suddenly filled the room, like an invisible airbag.

'Pardon?' I said, not for the first time. My dad also seemed taken aback by the turn of conversation: for once, I realised, he wasn't trying to milk it.

'Well,' he said, recovering slightly, 'When I say we play bowls, I don't mean on the same team because the men's team and the ladies' team are two separate things, but we both play at the same club... Not that she's been in much lately. But then she is getting on a bit – in fact there was talk of someone going round to see if she was all right.'

'You know Cora Vanstone?' I said.

'Yes,' said my dad, 'I just told you.'

'Fuck,' I said.

'Don't swear, Robert,' said my dad.

This wasn't good news. It linked me with Cora Vanstone in a way that I didn't feel comfortable with. Then again, my dad's connection – if, of course, it was a real connection – could be useful, although I had no idea how. Either way, it was all very confusing. I decided to have a shower and think about it later. I went upstairs to deal with the pipes of hell, leaving my dad to clear the breakfast things.

When I came downstairs, the kitchen was tidy and my dad was sitting at the table with a photo album.

'Look,' he said as I sat down, and pointed at a large colour photo of a lot of people sitting at a long dinner table. 'That's from the Bowls Club Christmas luncheon two years ago. See, there's me, there's Will Moulton whose son you were at school with... and there's Cora Vanstone.'

He pointed at the photo. I leaned forward for a better look.

'That's not Cora Vanstone,' I said.

Now it was my dad's turn to look.

'Yes it is,' he said. 'I'd know her anywhere. I mean, I do know her. I was sitting two seats away from her. That's definitely Cora Vanstone.'

He pushed the album towards me. I looked again but I really didn't need to. If the woman in the photograph was Cora Vanstone, then one thing was clear: the woman I had met was not. The Cora in the photograph was a biggish woman, unlike the woman I had met, who was small and bird–like. This Cora was younger too, in her sixties, unlike the other Cora, who might even be eighty. And this Cora looked friendly, the kind of person who might be outgoing and even jolly: nothing like the wraith-like woman in the vintage Rolls–Royce. There was no doubt: they were as different as chalk and chewing gum.

My dad peered at the photograph, as if looking for a clue in the other Cora Vanstone's – the real Cora Vanstone's – eyes.

'I like Cora,' he said. 'She drinks too much and she goes on about her dog all the time, but she's a good sort. Rattles around that big house on her own, poor thing, now that her husband's gone. Jim, he was the bowls player, really, but when he died, Cora kept coming for the company.'

He looked at me, as seriously as a dad can look at someone, which is very seriously.

'If she's missing, you need to do something about it, Robert.'

I ignored the name thing and said, 'Me? Why me?'

'I could do it myself, I suppose. Although I'm not as – you know – as I used to be.'

I looked at my dad. For the first time, I saw him as he saw himself – an old crock, not too steady on his feet. To me, he was a rock, indestructible, but I could see how absurd that was. Then again, he was more solid than me. Here I was, quite prepared to run away and forget all about this business. My dad was seriously considering conducting a single-handed manhunt just because he used to play bowls with an old woman who talked about her dog too much.

I felt, if not shame, then a close cousin to shame. So what if armed men had been pursuing me? They hadn't actually shot me. What if I was the possessor of a rare historical document (I hadn't forgotten the scrap of paper in my wallet)? They had the rest of Cora's note-book. Surely they were finished with their task now. Whatever. I knew what I had to do. I had to sort this out.

'You're right,' I said to my dad. 'It is on me. Whatever's going on, I need to sort it out. Who knows, I might even meet Penelope again.'

'Women,' said my dad. 'It's always the women with you.'

I ignored this too. 'How far is Cora Vanstone's from here?'

'Palmer House?' he said. 'Bit of a drive. Other side of Exeter. Here, I'll draw you a map.'

'I've got satnav, Dad.'

'I'll draw you a map,' he said, more firmly this time. 'I don't want you driving through a supermarket like that chap in Germany.'

And off he went. He came back a few minutes later with a hand-drawn map and a shoebox.

'Here,' he said. I took the map – it had about three lines on it and even fewer words – and opened the shoebox. Inside was a massive great gun.

'It's a Webley service revolver,' said my dad. 'It's cleaned and loaded.'

'Where the hell did you get –' I said.

'Came with the cottage,' said my dad, looking shifty. 'And thank goodness, eh? You can't be too careful these days.'

'I've never fired a gun in my life,' I said.

'Yes you have,' said my dad, looking hurt. 'When we stayed in Scotland, on that farm.'

A dim memory returned of me, at thirteen, shooting an air pistol on a firing range somewhere in Aberdeenshire.

'Oh right,' I said. 'I should be fine with this then. Dad, I can't believe you've just given me a gun.'

'I can't believe you're not called Robert,' said my dad, his talent for not dropping anything very much to the fore. 'Are you sure you don't want me to come with you?' he added.

For a moment I imagined my dad and me sneaking up on a gang of footpads, pistols at the ready.

'Quite sure,' I said. 'I need you here in case…'

'In case what?' said my dad.

'In case I need you.'

If Dad found my logic circular, he didn't say anything. He just put the lid back on the shoebox and said, 'I'll make you some sandwiches and a flask,' and went back to the fridge. I headed upstairs and got my things together. When I returned, there were a Tupperware box and a tartan Thermos on the table, along with the shoebox, the bag of old cassettes, and the largest torch in the world. It was the size of a teenager's arm. This time, I didn't ask my dad where he'd got it from.

My dad helped me carry everything to the car and watched while I set up the satnav, refraining entirely from shaking his head at this newfangled airy-fairy nonsense. I got out of the car, expecting a wooden hug. My dad put his arms around me.

'Stay safe, son,' he said.

'I'll do my best,' I said, and hugged him tighter.

He let go hurriedly and stepped back. I smiled at him and got in the car. The Jag started first time, which was a relief as I was a bit emotional and I was sure Dad was feeling the same way. I could see him waving as I pulled out of the drive. Just before I turned into the lane outside the gate, I distinctly heard him shout, 'Charlie's a stupid name!'

Now that I was on the road again, actuality returned to me. I was no longer on an adventure, seeking to help a woman in danger. I was just a man in a hired car, with a gun in a shoebox that he would clearly never be able to use. The cold morning sun made everything seem hyper-real and I felt neither brave nor useful. The satnav told me that we were an hour and a half from East Budleigh and, I noticed, five miles from Crediton. I had never been to Crediton but I did know a limerick about it. Suddenly I found myself reciting to an empty car:

> 'There was a young gourmet of Crediton
> Who took pate de foie gras and spread it on
> A chocolate biscuit:
> He said, "By God, I'll risk it."
> His grave bears the date that he said it on.'

I stopped. I appeared to be losing my mind. This was entirely possible, I realised, but it was also to be avoided. With my free hand, I opened the box of cassettes and fumbled out the first one I had touched. I fitted it into the Jag's tape player and after a few seconds, the John Peel show theme – known to fans under its real name of 'Pickin' the Blues' by Grinderswitch – twanged out of the speakers. I sat back in my seat and began to relax. At least I could rely on familiarity to calm me down.

'Well, good evening fun-seekers, I hope you all had a rollicking Christmas...'

I froze in my seat. I couldn't believe it. Well, I could, because it was real, but even so. The first tape I'd taken from the box – the box I didn't remember ordering (probably because I'd gone on eBay drunk) – was a Festive Fifty. Not only that, judging by the tape quality (and the fact it was *on* tape) it was almost certainly an early Festive Fifty.

Maybe this was it. Maybe the first tape in the box was the one. The show all Peel collectors are mad keen to find. The one that should have turned up years ago.

I hadn't been entirely transparent with Penelope about the tapes. True, I was a fan of the shows and the music and Peel himself, but there was more to it than that. I was the victim of an obsession, an obsession that I shared with very few others. There are people out there, much more driven than I, who don't just collect old John Peel shows, or keep all their tapes: these people are encyclopaedists. Their aim is a simple but ambitious one – to track down, collect and make recordings of every single John Peel show ever. Naturally this is a monumental task, and equally naturally it is probably impossible, but that also makes the challenge more thrilling. Compared to these people, who haunt car boot sales and pester friends for their old cassette collections, I was an amateur.

It was hard work tracking down old Peel shows, but it had paid off. Years of shows had been discovered – the process obviously becoming easier with the increasing popularity of home recording devices like radio cassette recorders and, later, digital music. And there had been successes with the oldest material, too, as radio listeners who'd owned reel-to-reel tape machines had turned up recordings of 1960s Peel shows like *Top Gear* and *The Perfumed Garden*. But there were gaps, shows that should have turned up but hadn't. Some important sessions, for example. The odd show where Peel had played an important band's debut single.

And then there were the Festive Fifties. The Festive Fifty was probably the most-loved thing about the John Peel show. Each year Peel would compile a list – firstly on his own, then from listeners' votes – of fifty of the best songs of the year, or of all time, depending on which Festive Fifty you were listening to. And the Festive Fifties were – to many people anyway – important. They were a guide to changing musical tastes, to the shift in people's choices and, as this was the John Peel show, to what was considered new and exciting. Most famous of all was the Festive Fifty for 1977, which marked the earthquake shift from Peel's old listenership of album-based, 'dinosaur rock' to the speed, aggression and novelty of punk and new wave.

The 1977 Festive Fifty was, even for music fans who didn't like John Peel, an incredibly significant marker – and trigger – of a new moment in popular culture. But there was another thing about that particular Festive Fifty: nobody could find a recording of it. People knew what was in it, they could go and buy the songs from it, and reconstruct it for themselves. But for some reason, nobody in the world – *the world* – had a tape of it. Which, given that there were, as I said, recordings of Peel shows from the 1960s, is remarkable (the 1976 Festive Fifty is also missing, but for the reasons cited above, the Holy Grail is 1977). One Peel fan eventually tracked down an incomplete tape, so we can now hear the top thirteen records in the Festive Fifty. Another researcher found evidence that the 1977 Fifty was, bizarrely, made of sixty records: it's actually a Festive Sixty. But nobody had found the whole thing.

Yet.

I was sitting on the edge of my seat, listening intently over the tape hiss as Peel continued his introduction.

'…*been looking forward to this programme for many weeks now, because we're gonna start broadcasting tonight…*'

On one level, I didn't want to be the man to find it. There were other, more deserving Peel listeners, people who devoted all their spare time to copying tapes over to digital formats, who catalogued the contents of the shows online, and who surely deserved to find the show of shows. On another level, there was so little else in the world to discover that I would have been very happy to be the one who found it.

'…*the 1978 Festive Fifty, computed from your votes. Not that all of you voted, but a great number of you did.*'

Oh well. You can't have everything, I thought, and turned the Jag towards East Devon. At least 1978 was a great Festive Fifty, full of burning new sounds, with the old guard firmly booted out into the snow. I turned up the tape.

'…*But first I shall play you a few tracks from the Festive Fifty of 1976 by way perhaps of comparison. It is worth pointing out that four or five times as many people voted this year as did two years ago, when this was number 30…*'

Peel puts on a record with a psychedelic vibe. It's not the Sex Pistols, but it suits my disconnected mood, so I leave it on.

If I'm honest, I was a bit annoyed with my dad for raising the whole name thing. After all, I reasoned, I wasn't the only one. Take for example, plucked from the air, almost at random, the man I was listening to now, John Peel. Known to millions as 'Peelie', loved for Peel shows and Peel sessions and a variety of stages and rooms and events named in his memory, and he wasn't called John Peel at all. John Peel was born John Ravenscroft and changed his name when he became a DJ. He even changed his accent over the years, going from public schoolboy teenager to Liverpudlian when he moved to Texas and claimed that he knew The Beatles. But Peel was nothing compared to his former Radio One colleague, Tommy Vance, whose real name was Rick West. Except it wasn't. Rick West was his first DJ name, before he became Tommy Vance. His *real* real name was Richard Hope-Weston. Rick West (or Richard Hope-Weston) only became 'Tommy Vance' when he applied for a job at a radio station in Seattle and was told by the station's owners that his predecessor, the real Tommy Vance, had left in a hurry but, as they'd gone to the expense of having all his station idents made, which of course had his (the real Tommy Vance's) name in, that West or Hope-Weston would have to change his name to Tommy Vance. Which of course he did, meaning somewhat bizarrely that the false Tommy Vance went on to enjoy a long and success-ful career, while the real Tommy Vance disappeared into the mists of history.

All of which proves what? A name is a name is a name. End of story. I decided I'd dealt with my irritation and turned up what might in a different world have been called the John Ravenscroft Show. Then, five songs in – this being the Festive Fifty for 1976, some of these songs were pretty long – I noticed that my phone was ringing. The caller ID told me it was Armstrong. I took a deep breath, turned down 'Child in Time' and put him on speakerphone.

'Bread?' said Armstrong, using his considerable reserves of charm-lessness.

'Roger!' I said, brightly, because I knew he'd hate it. 'How are you?'

'The question is, Bread,' said Armstrong, '*where* are *you?*'

'On my way to Cora Vanstone's,' I said, surprised to be telling him the truth.

'Really?' Armstrong said. 'Because I've got Cora Vanstone here at the hotel and she's not happy.'

I thought quickly, my mind a powerhouse of bad logic and sputtering synapses. If Armstrong wasn't lying and I supposed he wasn't, then he was with either the real or the fake Cora Vanstone. If he was with the real Cora Vanstone then everything was fine and I could just drive into Exeter, meet them both and end this. But if he was with the fake Cora Vanstone, there was no way I was going near them. I felt like the man in the logic puzzle, where one twin is lying and the other one is telling the truth and the man has to come up with a question which will satisfy both situations. I thought quickly.

'In that case, I'll come to you at the hotel,' I said. 'I'll be there in about half an hour.'

'You'd better be,' said Armstrong, and rang off with the swiftness of long practice at being a dick.

I turned up the Festive Fifty again. The 1976 chart was still going on, with 'Strawberry Fields Forever' by The Beatles at 17. As John Lennon sang about no-one being in his tree, I checked the satnav. I was about ten minutes away. Not from the hotel, where I had no intention of going, but from Cora Vanstone's house. I had no idea what I would find when I got there but I was sure I'd find something. As for Armstrong, he could cool his heels. I wasn't sure what he was going to say to the fake Cora Vanstone and I didn't really care. I glanced at the satnav one more time and turned the Jag towards East Budleigh.

Devon is a very large county and as such it's home to many different Devons. There's the wild coast of North Devon, once the preserve of bosom-heaving literary temptresses and lifeboat emergencies, now a surfer's paradise for people who don't mind the fact that it's bleak and freezing. There's the much balmier South Devon, all palm trees and Gulf Stream breezes, with huge beaches and seaside resorts. There's Dartmoor, a fantastic collection of rock and gorse and very small ponies. And then there's East Devon, a place so picturesque you might think that it had been terraformed specially at the request of a post-card manufacturer. East Devon is so twee it makes Kent look macho. Everywhere you go, there are thatched cottages, whitewashed cart-wheels left artfully by roadsides, little bridges over babbling brooks, tea shops, tea rooms and country pubs with epic lunch menus and excessively strict lunch-serving hours.

The most East Devon-y place in East Devon is probably East Budleigh. Barely a hamlet, East Budleigh is, as its name suggests, mostly an annexe to the somewhat larger Budleigh Salterton, itself home to hundreds of former household names from the '70s, wealthy pensioners and people who've somehow managed, through good luck and reasonable health, not to end their days in retirement homes. Compared to the geriatric haven of Budleigh Salterton, East Budleigh is a less coherent place, being largely a scattering of farms, cottages, the odd chapel and possibly the least urban Chinese restaurant in the world outside of China itself. The whole thing looks like it should be populated by cartoon creatures in dungarees.

And then I saw it. The unofficial symbol of East Devon (and, to be fair, almost every coastal town in Britain). In its candy-striped trousers, its little weskit and its round, gazing eyes, idiot grin and black, black face. A golly.

If I had been a sociologist, or a cultural historian, I would have written a book about the golly. (I even had a name for the book: *The History of Mister Golly*.) Gollies have somehow become a totem for a whole section of the English population who (like almost every other section of the English population) consider themselves disenfranchised and cut out of society. Like a flipside to the St George's flag of bravery and nationalism, the golly (I'm using the shortened form) represents both a vanished past of nursery innocence that never existed and a resentful present where something that its owners tell us is a sweet and harmless toy has become a symbol of resentment and barely suppressed anger. The things creeped me out. All these shops run by sweet old ladies and all these retirement cottages inhabited by decent old couples who fought in wars, and in every single one there he was. I wouldn't have been surprised to find a golly nailed to a church door in some weird racially charged remake of *The Wicker Man*. Perhaps on Guy Fawkes Night they carried huge gollies through the streets and burnt them on bonfires.

The weird thing, or not so weird thing, was that I never knew anyone who had a golly as a child. I'm not sure my dad or his friends had them – they were on their way out long before my parents' generation came along – so they're not even nostalgia toys. They're a false memory or, more pertinently, a deliberately faked memory, a symbol of a time that never existed. I didn't, as you may have surmised, like them.

The one I was looking at now was smirking at me from the window of a little tea room, sitting at a miniature tea table with a porcelain doll, the kind that could roll its eyes, and a totally out-of-scale plastic troll with long green hair and no trousers. It was a nightmarish tableau. On the other hand,

I hadn't had any lunch and there was nowhere else open. I left my box of tapes in the car – I didn't want to examine the cassettes by hand, if that's what they were, because I wanted that thrill of sitting in the car and seeing, or rather hearing, if I'd found what I was looking for – and went into the tea room. A bell above the door dinged with silvery predictability and I walked in.

Immediately I felt as though I was a cowboy, walking into a Wild West saloon. There have been any number of comic scenes and sketches making the comparison between entering a tea room and pushing open a saloon door, from the film *Withnail and I* to the TV show *The Goodies*, and it's not hard to see why. Both situations are curiously similar – the stranger in town, going into a room full of potentially hostile people. The proprietor, whether it's a barkeep with an apron and a bottle of bourbon or an old dear with a teatowel, asking what'll it be or is there just the one of you? The stares from the cowhands or the retired RAF boys at the next table. And always that feeling that you just don't belong.

I scooped up the golly from the window and riddled it with bullets. Of course I didn't. I said, 'Just me, yes,' and sat at a table by the toilet, in accordance with the first law of tea rooms which is that, if you shouldn't be there, you have to sit by the bogs.

The old dear brought me a menu which was, in accordance with the laws of the tea room, a leather rectangle framing the actual menu which was also under a sheet of clear plastic. She indicated the specials, which were printed on a tiny card next to the sugar bowl and hinted at the existence of a cake trolley. I ordered a cream tea without looking at the menu and settled back to stare out the golly. I remembered reading a news story which claimed that British soldiers stationed in an unnamed Arabian country in the 1960s wore a golly badge for each Arab they had killed. I wondered, if this were true, if the soldiers had had to send off for each golly badge (they were only available from a jam manufacturer), which would mean they'd have had to collect one token per golly from a jam jar, and then when they'd finally accumulated enough tokens, wait several weeks for each badge. It seemed an awful lot of fuss; then again, perhaps a kindly sergeant major had thought ahead and brought a box of golly badges with him.

'They're for sale,' said the old lady, as she set my cream tea down.

'I was just looking,' I said, and she gave me a look which suggested that she knew I was an undercover reporter from *Political Correctness Weekly*. I spread jam and cream on my scones and chewed at them morosely.

'Jam on first? That's not very Devonian,' said a voice. I looked up. It was her.

'Penelope,' I said, accurately.

'I was always told that people from Devon, or in Devon, I'm not sure, put the cream on first and then the jam,' she said.

'What are you doing here?' I said.

'And where have I been?' she replied. 'And why did I go? And how did I know you were here? All these questions.'

'I only asked one,' I said. 'But yes, all right, what you said.'

'I'm so sorry, Charlie,' she said. 'But I got a call from Greg –'

'Greg,' I said. I think I sounded upset. I may even have pouted.

'Yes, Greg,' she said. 'I've known him a long time. I knew him a long while before I met you. And... and I owe him. A lot.'

Now she was looking down at her hands, as though she was wondering what they were doing there. I couldn't think of anything to say that I was actually able to say.

'Would you like a scone?' I finally managed.

CHAPTER SIX

Mr Snapdriver: My next witness is the artiste known as Lucinda – a
Mrs Whiting.
(Everybody looks at the dwarf.)
Cocklecarrot (with heavy sarcasm): And, of course–
The Dwarf: Yes, she is my mother.
 – Beachcomber, 'The Case of The Red-Headed Dwarfs', part 11

After a lot of jam and clotted cream and the weakest tea I'd ever
drunk, I was feeling slightly better. I wasn't in the least happy with
Penelope's explanations: apparently Greg had called her and
demanded she see him, and then they'd had a massive argument and
after that it all got rather vague, Penelope asking me to believe that
she'd taken another train back to Devon to look for me and had then
been just sort of driving around (I hadn't noticed another car arrive)
and somehow she had found herself in East Budleigh – like you do
– and had seen me through the window of the tea room, staring at a
golly.

'I don't believe you,' I told Penelope.

'You don't have to,' she said. 'It doesn't make what I'm saying any
less true.'

'Or more,' I said, getting up to leave.

'Charlie,' said Penelope.

I stopped. She'd never used my name before. Besides, I hadn't got
the bill yet. Sighing, I went up to the counter and waited for the old
lady to stop messing around with some spoons out the back.

'Was everything all right?' she said as I handed over the readies.

'I don't know,' I said, and walked out. 'Well!' she actually said as I
opened the door with a weak ding and headed for the Jag.

Penelope was already there.

'This car's been resprayed,' she said.

'No it hasn't,' I said, quick as a flash.

'Look,' she said, and scraped a fingernail against the bonnet. Sure enough, there was a sliver of brown underneath the rich maroon.

'Can't blame them, I suppose,' she said, flicking a flake of paint away. 'Who wants a brown Jag?'

'Looks like nothing is what it seems,' I said, opening the car door. Without asking, Penelope opened the passenger door. I looked at her.

'What are you doing?' I said.

'We need to talk,' she said.

'What about your car?' I said.

'What car?' she answered. 'I hitched a lift.'

'To East Budleigh?'

'No. He was headed for London and then, like I say, I saw you and –'

'You saw me? From a car window? In East Budleigh? Whilst driving from Exeter to London?'

'You said "whilst",' said Penelope. 'Nobody says "whilst".'

She grinned. I gave up.

'Get in,' I said, resigned. She got in.

'Where are we going?' said Penelope.

'Never mind that,' I said. 'Just – just tell me what's going on.'

'Tell me where we're going first.'

I screamed inside. 'Forget it,' I said.

'Okay,' said Penelope, happily. 'Oh, more tapes?'

She grabbed the box of cassettes from my dad's house, pulled one out and put it in the player.

'What are you doing?' I said, angrily.

'Changing the tape,' she said. 'Ooh, proper music.'

Penelope started clapping her hands to the sound coming from the tape deck which, to my surprise, was very much not the usual scratchy guitar rock John Peel played.

'This is great,' she said. 'What is it?'

Her question was answered as Peel's voice came in. *I really do think this is excellent stuff, and I have to say, and I wasn't going to say anything about this, but to the handful of malcontents who felt that for some reason we shouldn't have the Pet Shop Boys on the programme, if I told you they*

122

were something like Ein Zwei Drei from Müllheim, you'd think they were wonderful...'

'Ooh,' said Penelope. 'I like the Pet Shop Boys.'

And for the next few minutes the car rang with the sound of Penelope's voice singing along with what Peel assured us was the Pet Shop Boys covering Bobby O's 'Try It (I'm in Love with a Married Man)'.

I wasn't sure if she saw the irony, but said nothing.

'We're here,' I said, as Penelope roared the last notes of the song. She stopped singing and looked up.

'Oh, wow,' she said. I thought that I understood what she meant. We were driving through the gates of a very pink house. The gravel drive, which was flanked by a small orchard on the left and an ornamental garden on the right, was long, and the house wasn't close, but it was so pink that it seemed to actually glow in the afternoon sunlight. It was pink like a strawberry ice cream, and unrelentingly so, from door to window frame, from ground floor to roof. This was quite possibly the pinkest thing I had ever seen, never mind the pinkest house.

'Pink, isn't it?' I said.

'I don't believe it,' said Penelope, which seemed a slight overreaction. But then, it was a very pink house.

I stopped the car a short distance from the house, slipped the cassette back into its box – I had no desire to hear Penelope ruin any more new-wave hits of the 1970s – and unfastened my seat belt. Penelope didn't move.

'Are you not coming?' I said.

'I'll stay here if you don't mind,' she said. She sounded a little tense. By now I supposed that I should be grateful she hadn't thrown open the door and leapt into the shrubbery. 'OK,' I said, and got out. I walked up the gravel drive – pink gravel, naturally – to the house, occasionally looking over my shoulder to check that she hadn't made a break for it (I'd put the car keys in my pocket, just in case).

I went up to the front door. There was a bell pull, but it was long rusted. I looked for a more modern doorbell and, not finding one, took hold of a metal lion's head thing and rapped it hard. The sound echoed around most of East Devon, and I swear I heard a flock of starlings take off in a nearby field. But from the house answer, as they used to say, came there none. I rapped a few more times with equal success.

I didn't really know what to do next, which is one of the problems with not having a plan. I thought of texting Cora Vanstone, but then realised I didn't know which Cora was which, and I had no desire to alert the false Cora to my plans. I decided to walk around the side of the house and see if anybody was about.

After a few minutes, I had circumnavigated the building, and was about to go and check out some outhouses when I saw that one of the downstairs windows was open. I thought about that for a minute, and then walked back to the car.

'Nobody in?' said Penelope cheerfully.

'No,' I said, 'but I'm not happy.'

'Well, you could always leave a note and come back tomorrow,' she said.

'I mean, I think something's wrong,' I said.

'I sort of got that,' she replied. 'I was hoping you were just going to leave it.'

'I can't leave it,' I said. 'I promised my dad.'

Penelope considered this. 'All right then,' she said. 'Let's go.' She opened the Jag's door and walked up the gravel path. I locked the Jag and caught her up. We went round the back of the house and I was about to show her the open window when I realised that it was no longer open. I explained this to Penelope and she frowned.

'It could just be a cleaner.'

'I knocked on the door, though. Several times. Loudly.'

'I know, I heard. People in Europe heard. But she might have been hoovering. With headphones on.'

'That doesn't sound likely.'

'Really? I do it. And my brother does it when he mows the lawn.'

I felt we were losing the thread of the conversation, so I said, 'Well, anyway, the window's closed, so someone's in there, so I'm going to go round and knock again.'

Penelope was silent for a few seconds. Quite a few seconds. Then she said, 'The person who lives here – is it very important that you find her?'

'I promised my dad,' I said.

'Nothing more serious than that,' said Penelope. 'OK then.'

And she strode off towards one of the outhouses. I stared after her, wondering what the hell was going on. She went into the outhouse and, after a great deal of banging and clattering, came out again with a ladder and some other things which, when she was closer, I saw were a hammer and a piece of oilcloth.

'Come on then,' said Penelope, all but dropping the ladder on my foot, and strode off towards the front of the house again.

'Why are we doing this?' I said, as I helped Penelope prop the ladder up against the standard–issue Greek–style front porch. 'We should be banging the door knocker.'

'Think about it,' she said, handing me the cloth and the hammer as she started to ascend the ladder. 'You banged the knocker and they closed the window. That means they don't want company.'

'Unless it's a cleaner,' I said, following her up the ladder.

Penelope stepped out onto the top of the porch. It was covered in dead leaves, conkers and pigeon crap, but it was also just below one of the front windows.

'What if there's someone in there?' I said, as she held the cloth over the window and smashed the glass with the hammer.

Penelope pushed the pane through and unlocked the window.

'There won't be,' she said. 'My aunt never uses this room.' She raised the window with a light grunt and stepped in.

'What did you say?' I said as I followed her.

Penelope was right. The room was dark and cold, and the furniture was covered in sheets. I had never seen this in real life and was pleased that it was an actual thing, but I was more angry with Penelope.

'This is your aunt's house?' I said.

'Yes,' she said, 'didn't I say?'

'You know you didn't,' I replied, trying to keep the rising fury from my voice. 'You didn't say anything.'

'I know,' she said. 'But you didn't tell me we were coming here.'

'If I'd known it was your aunt's house I would have,' I said, at the limits of my self–control.

'And,' she said, 'if I'd known we were going to my aunt's house I would have told you.'

'But I didn't know it was your aunt's house!' I found myself shouting.

'Well,' said Penelope. 'You do now.'

And, before I could strangle her, she opened the door and went out into the hall.

The house was silent. We went from room to room, starting with the upstairs rooms, but there was nobody in the bedrooms or the bathroom or the spare room. Downstairs was the same. There was an enormous living room full of sheeted furniture, a similar dining room, a kitchen, all empty.

'I don't have very good associations with this place right now,' said Penelope.

'Not fond of your aunt?' I asked.

'My aunt is lovely,' Penelope said. 'But this is where I met Greg.'

'Oh,' I said, brilliantly. 'Is he local then?'

'No he was –' She stopped. 'We haven't looked in the study,' she said, and pushed open a door. Inside, for a change, there were no dust sheets. Just an old roll–top desk with swivel chair, a small, battered armchair that looked like it was mostly occupied by small dogs and a portable TV on a low table. The top of the desk was covered in framed photographs. I stared at one, then picked it up.

'That's my aunt,' said Penelope, indicating a familiar-looking cheerful woman in her sixties. I took the photo from her. My hands were shaking. Standing next to the cheerful woman was a very familiar-looking man.

'And that's my dad,' I said.

Somebody once said that the thing about coincidences is that that's what they are. They're coincidences. There is no mystic significance to the fact that, say, President Lincoln had a secretary called Kennedy while President Kennedy had a secretary called Lincoln, or however that goes. Coincidences are remarkable precisely and only because they are coincidences. Therefore the fact that Penelope's aunt and my dad were friends was not in itself that remarkable. Somebody had to be Cora Vanstone's niece and my dad's son. At least, that was what I was trying to tell myself. The alternative conclusion – that I was being in some way set up by Penelope – seemed so unlikely, and if I was being honest, so unwelcome, that I would clutch at any straw to escape it.

Penelope was clearly feeling something similar, because she said, 'Have you brought me here to do me in?' She looked frightened, too, genuinely frightened. I decided to set aside my doubts, and said, 'No, really, I'm just as much in the dark as you are.'

'I doubt that,' she said.

'That's a bit harsh.'

'I didn't mean it like that.'

'How did you mean it, then?' I said, and I could hear my voice rising absurdly. 'You don't tell me what you're doing, you disappear for days on end, turn up again out of the blue and then you accuse me of…'

I stopped. Penelope, to my intense annoyance, was smiling.

'You look so serious when you're angry,' she said. She stepped closer to me.

'Well, this is a serious business,' I began. Penelope put her hands on my shoulders. I stopped.

'I think,' she said, 'that we –'

There was a loud bang, like a door slamming. I froze. Penelope dropped her hands in alarm.

'What was that?' she said.

I ran to the window just in time to see a motorbike appear on the gravel drive. Someone jumped up behind the rider and the two of them roared off.

'I don't think it was the cleaner,' I said.

'We were seconds behind them too,' said Penelope, pushing back the cover on the roll–top desk. I couldn't work out what she meant at first, but then I saw it. One of the smaller drawers in the desk was open, and whatever had been in it was missing.

'I take it your aunt didn't have a safe?'

'Doesn't,' said Penelope. 'She's not dead, I hope. And no, she doesn't have a safe. Why, what's missing?'

'I'm guessing the notebook,' I said. 'The thing I came down here to see in the first place. Without the actual notebook, I can't determine if the manuscript, or whatever it is, is by JM Barrie or Daisy Ashford. Of course,' I added hastily, seeing the expression on Penelope's face, 'our real priority is finding your aunt.'

'Well, we know she's not here,' Penelope said, 'and we've no way of catching whoever those two men are. So we're stuffed.'

'Not necessarily,' I said. 'I'm supposed to be meeting Cora Vanstone right about now. The other Cora Vanstone, that is, not your aunt.'

'I see,' said Penelope, which was kind of her. 'I think I'd like to meet this other Cora. Where is she?'

'She's at my boss's hotel,' I said.

Penelope's face was expressionless. 'Do you think he's in on it?' she said.

'In on what?' I said. 'That's the question. And besides, why *would* he send me down to Devon to look at a manuscript and then steal it? That makes no sense.'

She considered this. 'I suppose so,' she said.

'Look,' I said, 'I know Roger Armstrong. He's a shit. A bad-tempered shit. But he's got Pring's interests at heart, and –' I thought of the Rawley Vulcan, '– frankly, he wouldn't even care if something was a fake or not if he could sell it. But he is very concerned with the firm's reputation.'

'These bastards always are,' said Penelope with surprising feeling.

'Armstrong doesn't care about what's right or what's legal,' I said. 'If we can persuade this other Cora that the jig is up, we can hold the police over her head until she tells us what's happened to – where your aunt is.'

'I can't believe you said "the jig is up",' said Penelope.

'It's a perfectly normal expression,' I said. 'What about my plan?'

'Why not?' she said. 'Let's go.'

The Jag sped out of the drive, up a country lane, and nearly rammed itself into the back of a tractor. I considered honking at it, but there seemed no point, as the lane was so narrow that it kept knocking large hanks of straw out of the bales on the back of the tractor. I texted Armstrong to let him know I was on my way, while Penelope passed the time by going through my stuff.

'What is this?' she said, pulling out the revolver my dad had given me.

'My dad,' I explained.

'Wow,' she said. 'Is it loaded?'

'No idea,' I said, but Penelope wasn't listening. She did something to the barrel and the gun fell in half. 'It's loaded,' she said, and clicked the bullet bit back into place.

'Why does everyone know about guns apart from me?' I said.

'I would say,' Penelope began cautiously, 'that someone who gives you a loaded pistol knows very little at all about guns.' She put the Webley in her bag.

'Put that back,' I said.

'And have the safety come off when we get a bump?' she said. 'No way. I'm not dying in a hail of bullets because you went too fast over a cattle grid.'

I saw her point. Meanwhile, the tractor had slowed down even further because – amazingly – a flock of sheep was now straying in front of it.

'Can this thing go over fields?' said Penelope.

'I doubt it,' I said. 'I think Ivor said the chassis has already fallen out once.'

The tractor driver was now honking his horn at the man in charge of the sheep, who was shrugging in a 'what can I do?' kind of way. My phone rang.

'Bread,' said Armstrong. 'Where are you?'

'I'm stuck in traffic,' I said, truthfully.

'Well, you've blown it,' he said.

'In what way?' I said, puzzled.

'Miss Vanstone,' said Armstrong, in tones that suggested he hadn't entirely hit it off with the old fraud, 'has other business to attend to.'

'Has she gone home?' I said, wondering if that would mean she was on her way to the pink house, then remembering that she wasn't the real Cora so it was unlikely.

'No idea,' said Armstrong. 'To be honest, Bread, I'm starting to get sick of this whole business. You've been a model of incompetence – I don't know anyone else who could make such a botch job of just driving somewhere – while she's a nasty old cow. I'd wash my hands of the whole thing if there wasn't something in it for Pring's.'

'How much is there in it for Pring's?' I said, and wished I hadn't. I could almost hear the cold sarcasm building up in Armstrong's voice.

'More than you know,' he said. 'If there's nothing else, Bread, I'm going to catch the train back to London. I'll see you tomorrow.'

'You'll what?' I said, watching the sheep driver finally herd his flock into a field, and the tractor head off down a muddy side road. But he had rung off.

'Well, that was rude,' I began, but Penelope was tapping me on my shoulder, quite hard. As the sheep cleared out of the road, I could see what she was pointing at.

A vintage Rolls-Royce, making its way up the hill, its driver honking at stray sheep.

'Hold on,' I said, and slammed the Jag into reverse.

'There's a passing place just ahead,' Penelope said, alarmed, as we cannoned backwards down the narrow lane.

'Can't risk it,' I said. The Jag banged into a hedgerow. I spun the wheel, taking a chunk of earth with me, and hurtled off in reverse.

'What exactly are we doing?' said Penelope.

'See that car?' I said. 'It belongs to Cora Vanstone.'

'My aunt's got a Vauxhall Corsa,' said Penelope. 'Oh, I see. That Cora Vanstone.'

'Yes,' I said, reversing all the way round a signpost marked COLATON RALEIGH, 'that Cora Vanstone.'

I shoved the Jag backwards into a pub car park seconds before the Rolls-Royce rounded the bend.

'Now what?' said Penelope, not for the first time.

'I don't know,' I said.

'We should follow them. That old cow is pretending to be my aunt. I want a word.'

'I'm not sure that's a good idea.'

'Just drive,' said Penelope. 'And put the Pet Shop Boys back on. I liked that tape.'

'*And now what I suspect is a first for this show, a cover of a Village People song – the last from them tonight, the Pet Shop Boys, performing Go West.*'

'I love this song!' said Penelope.

'So do I,' I said.

'Really?' she said. 'I thought you were all punk rock and weird.'

'This song,' I said, as the opening chords turned into dance–floor thunder, 'is really interesting.'

'Oh, it's *interesting*.'

'Yes, actually,' I said, stung. 'Most emotional or powerful songs are supposed to be authentic, or soulful, or made by people with acoustic guitars and harmonicas and all that. But this is a cover – of a very tacky song – by two men playing machines. And it's more authentic than anything else I know. It's also very sad.'

'It sounds very jolly to me. Like that other one. "YMCA".'

'The original is, yes. The original is a big silly anthem about moving to San Francisco and the whole '70s gay lifestyle thing. But the cover isn't, because the Pet Shop Boys recorded it after the AIDS epidemic of the 1980s, which wiped out that generation of gay men. The Pet Shop Boys' version is a lament for a lost generation. It's beautiful.'

Penelope was silent for a moment.

'Well, now you've made me sad,' she said.

'I'm sorry,' I said. 'I should have added, it's a eulogy for a lost generation that's also a massive disco stomper.'

I turned it up and opened the car windows. Penelope sang along and we followed the Rolls–Royce, at a safe distance.

After an hour or so, Penelope said, 'I don't think they're stopping.'

I agreed. The Rolls had avoided the roads to Exeter and was now heading west.

'They're heading for Cornwall,' I said.

'I wonder why,' said Penelope.

'Perhaps they've got your aunt stashed there,' I suggested, and regretted it at once.

'Stashed?' said Penelope. 'She's not a folding table.'

'Sorry,' I said. 'I believe they're heading into Plymouth.'

The Rolls had come off the main road and was driving along the Plym estuary.

'Oh look, a Greek temple,' said Penelope, pointing at a small round building on the other side of the water.

'Victorian folly,' I corrected.

'Whatever,' said Penelope. 'Do you think they're stopping in Plymouth?'

'I hope so,' I said. 'I feel like we've been driving for ever.'

'There's a burnt-out church in the middle of that roundabout,' said Penelope. 'This is a weird city.'

'Charles Church,' I said.

'I get the feeling you've been here before,' said Penelope. 'Wow, that sign says CITY CENTRE and OTHER CITY CENTRE. How can there be two city centres?'

I was about to speak when she gave me a look. 'Please don't tell me,' she said, 'I can't take much more explaining.'

I decided to give her the silent treatment. It didn't really work because she kept talking anyway.

'There's a bridge,' she said. 'I bet it's a Brunel.'

I said nothing.

'I knew it!' said Penelope. 'Oh, they're going across it.'

I swung the Jag into the same lane as the Rolls-Royce and we made our way across the Tamar into Cornwall.

'This is exciting,' said Penelope as we passed through yet another identical and unrustic Cornish village.

I nodded. I was getting tired now and, as night was falling, longed for a break.

'Hey!' Penelope suddenly shouted. I opened my eyes. I had fallen asleep for a second and was veering across the road somewhat.

'I need a break,' I said.

'I can't drive,' said Penelope. 'Sorry.'

I opened the driver's side window. Cold air flowed in. I felt a little better.

A few minutes later, Penelope said, 'I think they're pulling in.'

The Rolls was indeed leaving the road. We followed it into a large car park.

'Looks like they're staying the night,' said Penelope as Hodge went to the Rolls' boot and pulled out some bags. 'I can't tell if this is a pub or a hotel.'

I peered out of the window.

'It's a Three For One Inn,' I said.

We waited in the Jag for a few more minutes to be sure that Hodge and the false Cora had gone to their rooms, and then went into the Inn ourselves. This Inn was the same as the others – identical decor, menu and, so far as I could see, staff – but also offered accommodation. Penelope found the receptionist.

'We'd like a room for the night,' she said. I didn't say anything.

'Mr and Mrs Smith,' she added, and grinned at me. I didn't say anything again.

The receptionist handed her a key and told us where our room was. Penelope and I went up a small flight of stairs, as quietly as possible, in case Hodge and Vanstone were roaming the landing. Penelope opened the door and turned on the light. The bulb clinked off into darkness.

'Good start,' she said, and turned on a side lamp, which dimly revealed the room to be fairly small, and almost entirely dominated by a huge double bed.

'I'm knackered,' said Penelope. 'I'm going to have a shower, you see if there's a minibar.'

And she disappeared into the bathroom.

There used to be an etiquette for this sort of situation. The man would offer to sleep on the couch, or the floor or, in the days when baths were designed for lying in and not catching the water from the shower, in the bath. The only time a man and a woman would be compelled to share a bed was if they were either married to one another or handcuffed to one another. I looked at the floor doubtfully. Even aside from the poor state of the carpet, there was hardly enough room for a thin dog to lie down, let alone an adult human.

I liked Penelope a lot. She was very desirable. I fancied her. There was no ambiguity there. I had no idea how she felt about me, although she had spent a lot of time following me around the country. Then again, maybe she was just enjoying the adventure. Also, from my point of view, there was the issue of Greg. Penelope was still involved with him, and he seemed to be both awful and married. This didn't exactly put me off Penelope, but it made me feel even more awkward. Coupled with the fact that over the past three years, for reasons I shan't go into, I'd spent most of my time in the company of men and men only, I would have been a lot happier if we'd booked separate rooms.

Penelope returned in a T-shirt and not much else.

'Where's my drink?' she said. 'Honestly.'

She found a minibar somewhere in a wardrobe, brought out two miniatures of whisky and handed me one.

'I bet you feel awkward about this,' she said.

I thought about it.

'I think the whisky is helping,' I said.

'You haven't drunk any yet,' she pointed out.

I looked at her. I grinned. She grinned back.

'Down in one?' she said.

'Down in one,' I agreed.

'And then?'

I looked at her. She had the most beautiful smile I had ever seen.

'Oh God,' I said, with feeling. 'I can't believe I'm going to say this. But – you don't know me. I don't know you either, true, but I don't feel we should – maybe if you knew me – I really don't know.'

Penelope was silent.

'I'm sorry,' I said. 'Am I making any sense at all?'

Penelope continued to say nothing. Her eyes were tight shut, and for a moment I thought I had upset her. Then she let out a small snore and I realised that she had, suddenly and without warning, fallen fast asleep.

'Actions speak louder than words,' I told the wall, and pulled a cover over her.

The next day I woke to find Penelope in the shower. I went to the window to see where we were. There was a thick mist over the car park and the nearby woods, so I guessed we might be near the sea. I couldn't see anything else, so I had a look around the room for a kettle. Which is when I saw the mural.

'Look at that,' I said to Penelope as she came out of the bathroom.

'Good morning to you,' said Penelope. 'Look at what? Oh my.'

She studied the mural, which took up the entire wall behind the huge double bed.

'That's very dramatic,' she said.

'It's a Lenkiewicz,' I said.

'It's mad,' she said.

'The two are not incompatible,' I said, and went on to explain Lenkiewicz's extraordinary life and work. Penelope was interested, but somewhat shocked to hear that he had kept his model's corpse in a freezer.

'Why did he do that?' she asked.

'The man was called Edwin Mackenzie. He was Lenkiewicz's favourite life model,' I said. 'Lenkiewicz called him Diogenes because, when they met, Mackenzie was living in a barrel.'

Penelope gave me a very strong look. 'Please don't tell me anything else.'

I decided not to mention Gus Honeybun. Penelope saw my determined-to-say-no-more face and relented.

'I suppose he's quite popular round these parts,' she said. 'What with the Plymouth connection and all.'

'He is,' I said. 'He spent a lot of time in Cornwall as well, pretending to be dead.'

'I beg your pardon?' Penelope said.

'He was friends with a local peer,' I explained, 'Lord Eliot, for whom he painted the original of this mural. This is a copy.'

'No, really?' said Penelope. 'I thought all the great artists displayed their best work in Three For One Inns.'

'Ha,' I said. 'Anyway, Lenkiewicz and Lord Eliot were great chums, so when Lenkiewicz decided to explore the concept of death, he went into hiding at Port Eliot.'

'Is there a kettle?' said Penelope. 'This is early even for you, explanation-wise.'

I ignored this remark and followed Penelope into the bathroom as she filled a tiny white plastic kettle.

'Look at this,' she said, 'I think a doll must have left it behind. Poor doll, she must be parched.'

'Lenkiewicz was obsessed with death,' I went on doggedly. 'But as he couldn't know what it was like to be dead, he did the next best thing.'

'Did he listen to you explaining things?' said Penelope sweetly.

'He faked his own death,' I said. 'He moved into Port Eliot and let everyone think he was dead.'

'Wow,' said Penelope. 'Do you want sugar or will this sweetener stuff do?'

I could see I was losing her.

'I thought you'd be interested,' I said, huffily.

'I slept with you, isn't that interested enough?' said Penelope.

I was about to draw her towards me when I heard something outside. Familiar voices.

'It's them,' I said. 'Hodge and the false Cora. And they're on their way out.'

'I think we're okay,' said Penelope. 'The breakfasts here look massive.'

Penelope was right. We had time to check out and wait in the Jag before Vanstone and Hodge were even in the Rolls. As they finally began to pull out of the car park, I crammed a shortbread biscuit in my mouth and followed.

'Where are we anyway?' she said.

'We're somewhere near Fowey,' I replied.

'Foy?' said Penelope. 'I can't see it on my phone.'

I spelled it for her.

'I give up,' she said. 'Nothing's ever the right way up with you.'

'Pardon?' I said.

'It's a thing my grandmother used to say,' Penelope said. 'I mean, not about you specifically, obviously. Just in general. But it's true. Nothing is the right way up with you.'

'I don't know what you mean,' I said.

'Don't tense up,' said Penelope. 'Yes, you do. With your – your tapes of MP3s, and your weird facts and your antique whispering and your –'

'My what?' I said. I was actually quite tense now, but I wasn't going to admit it.

'Your name,' she said. 'I've never met anyone called Bread before.'

'I've never met anyone called Penelope before,' I said. Even as I said it, I could see it was mistake.

'Penelope is a name. It's a woman's name,' said Penelope. 'Bread is a food's name.'

'And it's my name,' I said, rallying. 'It's my last name. Come to think of it,' I added, 'I don't even know your last name.'

'Oh look,' said Penelope. 'The Rolls is turning onto that big road.'

We drove down the A30, our only accompaniment the radio (Penelope had requested a break from John Peel). The Rolls was a safe distance ahead, obscured partly from our view by a couple of caravans and an Ocado truck.

'What if they turn off?' said Penelope.

'Then we'll see them,' I said. 'Besides, they won't. This is pretty much the last road in England. Once we get past Hayle, there's nothing but the A30 all the way to Mousehole.'

'Mowzell?' said Penelope.

'Mousehole,' I said.

It went a bit quiet after that. We overtook a caravan and the Ocado truck turned off for Camborne.

An hour passed in the level company of Classic FM. During the ad break, Penelope suddenly grabbed my wrist.

'Look,' she said.

I looked but couldn't see anything.

'Behind us!' she almost shouted.

I looked in the rear–view mirror. A few cars behind was the white Prius.

'Is it them?' I said.

'I don't know,' she said. 'But it's the same colour and everything.'

'Well, there's nothing we can do,' I said. 'We just have to keep going.'

'How did they know we were here?' Penelope said, sounding worried.

'No idea,' I said. 'Maybe we should search the car for tracking devices.'

'Are you serious?'

'It's possible.'

'But why would they be tracking us? What do they want you for?'

'I haven't the faintest,' I said, which wasn't strictly true. I didn't know what they wanted, specifically, but I was sure that it had something to do with either the Barrie notebook or the Rawley Vulcan and possibly, although I couldn't see how, both. Either way I wasn't best pleased.

'I've got an idea,' said Penelope. 'Pull over now.'

'What, by the side of the road?'

'No, in the sky. Yes, by the side of the road.'

I did so, shaking my head. Penelope waited until the white Prius had passed us. The occupants didn't so much as look at us but it was the same two men.

'Now pull out,' said Penelope when the Prius was a few cars ahead.

'We're behind both cars now,' I said.

'Exactly,' said Penelope. 'Nobody's following us and we're following everyone.'

'But what if one of them suddenly pulls off into a B-road?'

'Then if it's the Rolls we follow it, and if it's the Prius, we don't.'

I had to admire her logic.

'Tell me it's a good plan.'

'It's a good plan.'

'*Thank* you. Would you like me to put on a tape?'

'Well, hello there once again. This final programme in our two-week potter through the best of British rock concerns itself, not unnaturally, with The Beatles.'

'Pet Shop Boys, Beatles… it's quite good, this show, isn't it?'

I said nothing. Despite the hour, it was getting darker outside and – while I was aware that this was merely a feeling – the land was getting narrower. England was tapering off all around us, with two coasts scarcely a few miles from each other, and in front of us, the entire Atlantic Ocean.

'Yes,' I managed to reply finally, 'It is quite good.'

'So did he like The Beatles, then, John Peel?'

'He knew John Lennon quite well. He used to make tapes for Lennon and send them to him and Yoko in New York.'

'I wonder if he sent him this one.'

I looked at Penelope. In this light it was hard to tell if she was joking or not.

'I doubt it,' I said, and turned the sound up. John Peel was listing chart statistics.

'This is a weird show,' Penelope said. 'He's not talking much, is he? He's just introducing the songs like a proper DJ.'

'I think he's bored,' I replied politely. 'This is the worst era for the show. Music is really dull, there's nothing new, and he's reduced to these round-ups of the past. All his shows are retrospectives.'

'I hope things improve for him,' Penelope said cheerfully.

'Oh, there's something big around the corner,' I said, aware that I sounded more smug than knowledgeable.

'I bet it's punk,' said Penelope. 'It's always punk.'

'I Saw Her Standing There' ended with a crash.

'I always had a lot of time for that actually,' says Peel. *'Mainly because when I started working as a groovy DJ in America and was supposed to talk with a Liverpool accent, I found that 'one! two! three! four!' very helpful. Uh, a couple of Ringo's hits for you now...'*

It was afternoon in Cornwall now. A continuous if sparse stream of traffic was making its way west to Penzance and points beyond. Ahead of us, I could still make out both the Rolls and the white Prius. I had no idea if the occupants of either car knew we were there.

Penelope yawned. 'Is it bedtime yet?' she said. 'I ask because I'm tired.'

'We've only just missed lunchtime,' I said.

'Then I'm going to have to say it,' she said.

'What?'

Penelope looked at me and grinned.

'Are we nearly there yet?'

Time passed, as time tends to. The miles rolled away under the Jag's wheels with no sense of any actual distance having been travelled. We passed signs for towns and villages, the occasional tor and some abandoned tin mines.

'We really are going all the way,' said Penelope.

'I'll say,' I said. 'The petrol capacity of the Rolls must be immense.'

'In books those things are always pulling in at quaint country garages,' Penelope said.

'I wish they would,' I replied. 'I need a wee and a pasty.'

'Nice combination,' said Penelope. 'Oh look, a red kite.'

We got stuck behind a minibus for a bit, which was a diversion. Some teenage boys gave us the finger.

'I miss V signs,' I said.

'What's a V sign?' said Penelope.

I gave her an old-fashioned look.

'I need the toilet now,' Penelope said.

'There's nothing I can do about that.'

'I know, I was just telling you. Oh wow, a country garage. And they're pulling in.'

'Right.'

I slowed down.

'We're going to wait until they're about to leave, then stop, have a toilet break, and follow them again.'

'Isn't that a bit risky?'

'Maybe. But no human body could withstand the pressures I'm dealing with right now.'

'OK.'

The white Prius slowed down as it passed the garage, then pulled over.

'That proves it,' said Penelope. 'They're following the Rolls too. Good job you've got your gun.'

'Yes,' I said, not feeling convinced.

Hodge got back in the Rolls. I slowed as he pulled out.

'I can't believe they didn't have a toilet.'

'I can't believe you went behind the carwash.'

'You did, I don't see why I shouldn't.'

'Can you still see the Rolls?'

'Yes, and the Prius is behind it.'

'I wish I'd got a pasty.'

It was getting properly dark now. We were heading down winding lanes, past lowering tors and, more and more frequently, the Atlantic would suddenly appear over a headland for a moment and vanish again. After a while there was nothing but darkness, and headlights.

'Where are we?' Penelope asked.

'Near the end,' I said.

'That's a bit dramatic,' she said. 'Of the world?'

'Might be,' I replied.

Lights loomed out of the darkness above us.

'Oh, we're somewhere,' said Penelope.

The lights separated out into windows. Ahead of us was a large house, yellow in the evening lamplight. It had a castle-like roof with pretty crenellations and looked extremely posh, especially considering its location in rugged Cornish farmland.

'Stop driving now,' said Penelope. 'We're almost on top of them.'

She was right. The road was now tight and winding, surrounded by high, claustrophobic banks of earth and foliage, but it was indented, as if grudgingly, with passing places, some of them large enough to park a tractor. One was coming up, so I pulled into it and killed the engine and the lights.

We watched in darkness as the Rolls went up the drive.

A few seconds later, the Prius drove past the house.

'They'll be parking further along the road,' I said.

'Or driving to America,' Penelope said. 'Look where we are.'

I got out of the car in the dark. After a moment I could hear waves and the jangle of bells on buoys.

Penelope got out of the Jag and clambered onto the roof.

'Hey,' I said, 'this isn't my car.'

'It's not mine either,' she said. 'Come on up.'

I gingerly climbed on top of the Jag, praying we wouldn't go through the roof.

'Look,' she said.

On one side of the house there was land. On every other side was sea. Far away, the beam of a working lighthouse circled the night air.

'Where are we?' I said.

'Call yourself a local boy,' Penelope mocked.

'It's dark,' I pointed out.

'Finis terra,' said Penelope. 'Land's End.'

We waited half an hour. I resisted the urge to put on a Peel tape, and instead drummed my fingers on the steering wheel, until a look from Penelope silenced me.

There is something eerie about being at the far end of a country, especially when that end is a toe at the end of a leg on top of a hill. Behind us, like a straggling ribbon, was the rest of the country, itself isolated from the mass of the continent. Ahead of us and below us was the sea, a dark, cold, ranting mass of water that was far from inviting. The house was almost as forbidding, and seemed to look down on us in silent disapproval. Not even its fussy crenellations and pink walls – grey now in the near-darkness – could reduce the impression that this was a sour house, one that did not want us to be there.

We watched as the false Cora opened the door of the house, and Hodge followed her with the luggage from the Rolls-Royce. We waited a few more minutes for the two men in the white Prius to return, but they didn't.

'I can't sit out here all night,' Penelope said.

'All right,' I said. 'Time for action.'

'Wait,' Penelope said.

She leaned over and kissed me. It was an excellent kiss.

'Thanks,' I said.

She sighed. 'I knew you'd be a thanker,' she said.

'I don't know what you mean.'

We got out of the Jag. I remembered something and leaned in to pick up the gun, but Penelope took it off me.

'I'd better take this,' she said.

'I'm fine with it,' I said, but she put it in her pocket, where it bulged.

'All right then,' I said, miffed. 'What's the plan?'

'I haven't really got one.'

'OK then, let's just go in and shoot them.'

Penelope gave me a look.

'We can't do that, we don't know where my aunt is.'

'Of course. How foolish of me.'

We approached the gate. It was an enormous wrought-iron affair with a sign on it that said KILLIGREW HOUSE. I was about to push it open when Penelope stopped me.

'Let's go round the back.'

We walked down the lane for a while. The white Prius was nowhere in sight, but there was a small farm a few yards away, and outside it a local lad was trying to start his motorbike.

We kept close to the hedgerow and, after a minute or two, we arrived at a small wrought-iron gate set into a large brick wall. It was locked.

'We could climb over the wall,' I said dubiously. The wall was high, and studded with bits of broken glass.

'Hang on,' said Penelope, and took out the gun.

'What are you doing?'

'I'm going to shoot the lock off.'

'Won't that be quite loud? Maybe attract their attention?'

Penelope thought.

'Hang on,' she said.

We stood there for a few seconds. Then I said, 'What are we waiting for?'

'That,' said Penelope, as the farm boy roared past on his motorbike. As he did so, Penelope fired the gun at the lock. The lock sprang off.

'That was really loud,' I said.

'The noise of the motorbike covered it,' she said. 'They'll think it backfired.'

'Or they'll think someone was firing a gun.'

'Which do you think is more likely? They're not expecting gunshots. Anyway, this is the countryside. People are always firing things.'

I gave up. 'You've just used up our only ammo.'

She looked at me seriously. 'Nobody says "ammo",' she said.

I decided there was no point in arguing with her. Penelope threw the padlock into the hedge and pushed the gate. It didn't move.

'It's completely rusted,' she said.

'Maybe you could shoot the hinges off.'

'There's no need to be sarcastic.'

'Here,' I said, and gave it a shove. The gate moved. I shook it.

'Now who's making a noise?'

'Stand back.'

I shoulder-charged the gate. It hurt my shoulder, but the gate finally moved. Penelope opened it and we went in.

We were on a low slope. There was nothing between us and the house but some bushes. It was a moonless night and, save for the circling lamp of the lighthouse far out at sea, the entire area was steeped in darkness.

'I wish we'd brought a torch,' Penelope said.

'Use your phone,' I said.

And we crept up on the house, the light from our mobiles illuminating the ground in front of us in tiny grey rectangles.

We walked around the grounds. It was freezing cold, and coming on to rain. Lights were going on and off in the house, as though Hodge and Vanstone were going from room to room, checking the place was empty. Soon all the upstairs lights were out, and a short while after that, most of the downstairs lights.

'It's like someone left the lights on so they could find it,' Penelope said.

'Who, though?' I said.

'Whoever owns the place,' said Penelope.

'Maybe they do,' I suggested.

'I doubt it,' said Penelope. 'I generally find that people who have to go round pretending to be other people very rarely have a nice house of their own.'

I could see the truth in this.

'Well, they appear to have settled in,' I said. Certainly there had been no activity in the last few minutes that I could see.

'Now what do we do?' said Penelope. 'Funny, we come all this way and when we get here, we don't have any ideas.'

'I've got an idea,' I said. 'Don't look at me like that.'

'What is it?' said Penelope, with very little enthusiasm.

'Well –' I said.

'Is it that I go up to the front door as a diversion because they don't know me while you sneak in the back?'

'Yes,' I said, after a moment.

'Perhaps I could dress up as a postwoman.'

'Are you being sarcastic?'

Penelope grinned.

'I could go to the door,' she said. 'But what would you be doing?'

'Like you said,' I said. 'I'd sneak in the back.'

'Then what?'

'Then, I don't know, I'd let you in.'

'How? I'm round the front.'

'I could leave the back door open while you came round.'

'Then what?'

'Then we'd be in.'

'Then wh…'

'Stop saying that.'

The back door opened. Hodge stepped out and looked around. He didn't look happy. Then he stepped back inside.

'I bet he heard the gunshot,' I said.

'I bet he locked the back door,' said Penelope. 'I've got a plan, by the way.'

'What is it?'

She told me. I didn't like it.

Ten minutes later, having sneaked back out through the gate and made my way back to the lay-by, I found myself pointing the Jag up the drive for the second time that day. It was dark now, and my head-lights lit up the chrome and white paintwork of the Rolls-Royce like an enormous Christmas bauble.

I parked the Jag next to the Rolls-Royce, making the place look like a tiny vintage car rally, and walked up to the front door. I rapped the door knocker. After a minute, Hodge opened the door. If he was sur-prised to see me, he gave no indication. His face was solid and expres-sionless. He was still wearing his chauffeur's hat and uniform.

'Hello, Hodge,' I said.

'What are you doing here?'

'We followed you,' I said. 'What are you doing here?'

Hodge looked me squarely in the eye so I knew he was lying.

'Miss Vanstone lives here,' he said.

'Is Miss Vanstone at home?'

'No,' he said, 'she's gone for a run.'

I decided that this was sarcasm.

'Could you tell her that Charles Bread is here to see her?'

Hodge closed the door. Time passed. Then, just as I was starting to get cold on the doorstep, he opened it again, just wide enough to let me in. I squeezed past him into the hallway. He nodded at the study door and was about to close the door when I screamed at the top of my voice.

'My leg!' I shouted, for good measure, and fell to the floor clutching my shin like a footballer.

Hodge stood over me. He put his foot on my shin.

'There's nothing wrong with your leg,' he said.

'It's seized up,' I said. 'I'm in considerable pain.'

Hodge looked up at the ceiling. He muttered something under his breath – it was 'fuck' – and crouched down. As he did so, there was a faint clunk as the front door shut. Hodge shrugged, hoisted me to my feet and half dragged me to the study. He thumped on the door.

'Come in,' said the woman calling herself Cora Vanstone, and Hodge pushed me into the room. I hobbled to a chair and sat down.

'It's his leg,' said Hodge. 'He says.'

Cora Vanstone looked at me.

'It's feeling better already,' I said.

'What are you doing here?' she asked.

'He followed us,' said Hodge.

'Good,' she said. 'Do you have the scrap of paper?'

I had to think for a moment.

'Yes,' I said. 'Do you have the notebook?'

I felt I was being smart. Perhaps it was Hodge who'd taken it from the pink house. Maybe it was someone else. Either way, her reaction would be interesting. But I suspected that the fact she wanted the scrap of paper was interesting. It suggested that, not having the notebook, they were keen to get the nearest thing to it, which was at least proof of the notebook's existence – the scrap of paper torn out from the notebook.

Cora said nothing.

'Why do you need the scrap of paper when you have the notebook?' I said.

'I don't need it,' Cora said. 'But I would like to reunite it with the rest of the notebook. It is not yours and there is no reason for you to hold on to it now that we are together again.'

'About that,' I said. 'Last time we met, there were people shooting at us. How –'

Just then there was the most appalling crash. Hodge and I ran out into the hall. There in the middle of the room were the remains of a huge blue vase.

'There's something going on,' said Hodge. He fixed me with a most unpleasant look. 'I see your leg's got better.'

'There's no need to be rude, Hodge,' said Cora. 'Bring some drinks into the blue room – whisky, I think – while Mister Bread finds his bit of paper.'

'That's very kind,' I said, as she steered me into a room full of blue stuff. There was a Louis Something desk in the corner, still in use with pens and envelopes in it. After a moment's fiddling, I sealed an envelope and handed it to Cora Vanstone.

'I've sealed it for safe keeping,' I said. 'Until you're able to put it back in the notebook.'

Cora looked as if she were about to say something, but as she couldn't actually admit that she didn't have the notebook, she just thanked me and put the envelope in her handbag. I pulled up a blue chaise longue and we waited for Hodge to come in with the drinks, which he served with all the joy and fervour of a man who did not want to be serving anybody some drinks.

Conversation was sparse, to say the least. Vanstone was clearly waiting for Hodge to return while I had my own reasons for not revealing anything. Outside there was a faint thump.

'I think Hodge has dropped something,' I said.

Vanstone didn't reply.

'Nice hi-fi,' I added. There was an old music centre on a blue table in the corner. It was so old it had a turntable for vinyl and a cassette deck.

Another thump.

'Hodge?' called Cora, nervously I thought.

'Do you mind if I see it works?' I said and, to Vanstone's probable surprise, I got up and took the tape that Penelope had handed me earlier in the car out of my pocket and put it in the music centre.

'Young man,' said Cora, 'what are you doing?'

I pushed down the play button. The familiar sound of 'Pickin' the Blues' came out of the speakers.

'I must ask you to turn that down,' she said.

I turned it up.

Cora stood up, just as Hodge entered the room. He was holding a golf club.

'That's not a tray of drinks,' I said.

'What's going on?' said Hodge.

'Turn that off!' said Cora.

I turned it off and sat down.

'I'd really like a drink now,' I said.

Cora exchanged a glance with Hodge. Clearly neither of them were happy.

And then Penelope came in.

'I've searched the place,' she said. 'Nothing.'

Hodge and Vanstone looked suitably surprised.

'She must have got in when he was buggering about with his leg,' said Hodge.

'Who are you?' said Cora Vanstone.

'Penelope,' said Penelope. 'Who are you?'

I intervened, for my own entertainment.

'This is Cora Vanstone,' I said. Penelope raised an eyebrow.

'I live here,' said the false Cora.

Now it was my turn to be surprised.

'I thought you lived in East Budleigh,' I said.

'Yes,' she said. 'And I live here as well.'

'She's minted,' said Hodge. 'There's a clue in the Rolls-Royce.'

'This is a waste of time and these two are a pair of liars,' said Penelope. 'Come on, Charlie, we should be going now.'

'No, you don't,' said Hodge, blocking her way.

'If you have a problem, you should call the police,' Penelope said, pushing his golf club aside.

Hodge stopped. He looked at Cora, who shook her head.

'I'll tell Mister Armstrong about the missing notebook,' I said. 'I'm sure he'll be very interested.'

We walked out before Hodge could think of something violent to do.

Penelope and I hurried into the hall.

'There's no sign of my aunt anywhere,' she said. 'I didn't think there would be but I had to check.'

'Of course,' I said. 'Maybe now we do involve the police.'

'Well, we can file a missing persons report,' said Penelope, 'but I don't think that'll help. I say we go back in there.'

'You're right,' I said, remembering. 'I've left my tape in the music centre.'

'I meant go back and shoot one of them in the leg,' said Penelope, 'Get them to tell us where she is.'

'Oh, right,' I said. 'But what if they don't know?'

Penelope wasn't listening. She was looking over my shoulder, at the front door. I hadn't heard it open.

In the doorway stood two men, one thin, one round.

'Oh hello,' said the round man, 'would you like to take advantage of our three–for–one deal?'

And he knocked me down with the butt of his gun.

I was unconscious for a while after that, so I only have other people's accounts of what happened, which can be unreliable to say the least. But I have no reason to doubt the gist of the matter, which is that I was dragged by the other man from the white Prius into a large drawing room and dumped on a settee, while the other herded Penelope, Hodge and Cora Vanstone into the same room and trained his gun on them while they waited for me to recover consciousness.

I woke up for a minute, said, 'White Prius, I wanna Prius, white Prius, a Prius of my own,' and passed out again. This had the effect of briefly uniting everyone in confusion (I gathered from Penelope that the conversation had not been flowing while I was out cold).

I woke up for the second time a few minutes later with a headache, which at least had the effect of reminding me of the last time I'd been bashed on the head, namely in the doorway of a Three For One Inn.

The men from the white Prius had been present on that occasion too. Perhaps, I thought to myself, they had just been waiting to meet the person who bashed me on the head, namely Greg. Perhaps they'd been on a date night. Perhaps – I gave up thinking because it was starting to hurt, and I realised that I was still dizzy and confused from being struck. I sat up, discovered that Penelope was holding my hand, and tried to follow the conversation.

'Who are you?' Hodge was asking in a surly manner.

'Ask him,' said one of the men, indicating me with his gun.

'I'm asking you,' said Hodge, who clearly was not a man to let things lie.

'All right,' said the taller of the two men, a sardonic look on his face. 'My name's Foster. And this –' he said, indicating his rounder companion, '– is Mister Piano.'

'Piano?' said Hodge.

'Renzo Piano,' said the smaller man. 'And he's Norman Foster.'

'Really?' said Hodge.

'Why not?' said the man who called himself Foster. 'We're clearly the villains here.'

'What are you doing here?' Hodge asked.

'Isn't it obvious?' Foster said. 'We've been following him. Bread, or whatever his name is.'

'Ridiculous name,' said Piano.

'Why are you following him?' said Hodge.

'A little bird paid us to,' said Foster.

'Greg,' I said.

'No names, no pack drill,' said Piano.

'Anyway, we asked ourselves, why are we doing the little bird's work? We know what he wants, so why not take it for ourselves?' said Foster. 'And here we all are.'

'Sitting in a rainbow,' added Piano.

I must have still been dazed from the blow because none of this was making any sense to me.

'And what brings you here?' Foster asked Hodge.

'His name is Hodge and he works for me,' said the fake Cora Vanstone. 'My name is Cora Vanstone and this is my house.'

'No it isn't!' said Penelope.

'How do you know?' said Hodge, who was revealing a late-flowering gift for pedantry.

'I don't, for sure,' said Penelope. 'But I do know that she isn't Cora Vanstone.'

'Who's Cora Vanstone?' said Piano.

'My aunt,' said Penelope.

'I'm not your aunt,' said Cora. She turned to Foster. 'I have no idea who this young woman is.'

'Well, this is fun,' said Foster.

'Let's shoot someone in the arse,' said Piano, surprisingly.

I could sense a rising tension in the room.

'Wait,' I said. I stood up with some difficulty and addressed myself to the fake Cora. 'If this is your house,' I said to her, 'then who painted that?'

And I pointed to a large, colourful, chocolate-boxy portrait of a half-dressed young woman.

'My aunt loves that painting,' said Penelope.

'It's terrible,' Foster said.

'I like it,' said Piano.

Cora Vanstone looked confused.

'Yes,' I pressed, 'but who painted it?'

There was an awkward silence.

'Jack Vettriano,' said Hodge.

'No waiters,' said Piano, shaking his head.

'It's a Lenkiewicz,' I said. 'Devon artist.'

'Oh yes,' said Penelope, 'I see it now.'

Piano shook his head at Cora. He may even have tut-tutted.

Foster went up to the Lenkiewicz to have a closer look.

'Is it valuable?' said Foster.

'Fairly,' I said. 'Put it this way, people think they're worth faking.'

'Sincerest form of flattery, that is,' said Piano and moved towards the wall.

Foster gave him a 'not now' sort of look.

'Fair enough,' said Piano. 'I need a drink. Who's with me?'

'Right,' said Foster, a few minutes later when we all had drinks (Piano was a generous man with other people's liquor), 'let's start again.' He nodded at the fake Cora.

'Who are you?' he said.

'I told you,' she said, 'Cora Vanstone.'

'No, you're not,' said Penelope.

The fake Cora sighed. 'All right,' she said, in a distinctly West Country voice, 'I'm not. I'm called Mary Daventry. I'm an actor. So's he.'

Hodge shook his head. 'I'm more of a stuntman. I really was in the SAS.'

'With that gut?' sneered Foster. 'Catering Corps, more like. What's your real name, then? Sergeant Bollocks?'

'Hodges,' said Hodge. 'I'm not very good at making things up,' he explained.

Piano knocked back a large whisky in one.

'So why are two actors going round pretending to be an old biddy and her manservant, then?'

'We were hired by – someone,' said Mary Daventry, formerly Cora Vanstone. 'On the phone, we never met them. They just gave us a rough outline and told us to be these people. I didn't even know there was a real Cora Vanstone until I met him,' she added, nodding at me.

'Weird,' said Foster. 'I imagine whoever it was is after the same thing we are.'

'Do you know where my aunt is?' said Penelope.

'No idea,' said Mary Daventry. 'Sorry. We were just told get the notebook authenticated by him –' she nodded at me again '– and hand it over after. We were supposed to leave it at a hotel reception in Exeter.'

'What name?' Penelope said.

'Mister Da Vinci,' Mary Daventry replied.

'False name if ever I heard one,' said Hodge.

'Yes, I think we got that,' said Foster.

I could hear all this, but I couldn't really take it in. I suppose things tend to wash over you when you've been hit with the butt of a gun. I seemed to be floating above everyone, a feeling that was so real to me I was surprised nobody had commented on it.

Foster was still talking.

'How come you're here then?' he asked.

'Things got a bit out of hand,' Mary Daventry said.

'After you shot at us, we got another message to come down here and wait,' said Hodge.

'Wait for what?' said Penelope.

'We never shot at you,' said Foster.

'Yes you did,' said Hodge.

'Didn't,' said Piano. 'I'd remember something like that.'

There was a silence, as of some people trying to work out what the hell was going on.

'So where are we now?' Piano said.

'We get them to hand over the notebook and then we bugger off back to London,' said Foster.

'The notebook?' said Mary Daventry.

'Yes, the notebook,' said Foster who was definitely gaining a reputation for sarcasm.

'We don't have it,' said Hodge or Hodges. He seemed to find this funny.

'It's gone,' elaborated Mary Daventry.

'Is this true?' Foster asked me.

'Yes,' I said. 'I thought you took it.'

'If we'd got it, we wouldn't be here,' Piano pointed out. 'Wasting our time with you gits.'

'Well, if we haven't got it and they haven't got it...' said Foster.

'Maybe they have got it,' said Piano. 'Let's search them.'

'They haven't got it,' I said.

'Maybe you've got it,' said Piano, advancing towards me.

'We saw the person who took it,' Penelope said. 'So lay off, unless you get some weird kick out of searching people.'

'Not keen on it, to be frank,' said Piano. 'People often aren't clean where they should be.'

Foster stood up. 'This is a right pain,' he said. 'We've invested a lot of time in this.'

'Following these clowns,' agreed Piano.

I remembered something.

'Why did you keep approaching me?' I said. 'Why did you ask me about the Rawley Vulcan on that bus?'

'Keep you on your toes,' said Piano. 'Following people's more fun when they know you're on to them.'

'Besides,' said Foster, 'you caused a lot of trouble with that. Telling your boss it was a fake.'

A thought came to me. An unpleasant one.

'You're going to kill us,' I said.

'Not necessarily,' said Foster.

'Possibly,' said Piano. 'If you don't give us the notebook.'

'I told you, we haven't –' began Penelope.

'Worth a try,' said Piano, smiling horribly.

Foster looked at his watch.

'What?' he said suddenly.

'What do you mean, what?' said Piano.

'When I looked away then, at my watch,' said Foster, 'the old bat looked across the room at something.'

'Old trick,' said Piano. 'You pretend your attention's elsewhere, someone always looks where they don't want you to look.'

Foster had walked over to the table where Mary's handbag was. He took out the envelope.

'What's in here then?' he said to Mary Daventry.

She said nothing. He took out his gun.

'It's part of the notebook,' said Hodge or Hodges. 'The only bit we've got.'

'Worth something then,' said Foster, and put the envelope on the table.

'We're wasting our time here,' he said. 'We've got this, at least. Let's get out of here.'

'What about them?' asked Piano.

'Yeah, what about them?' said Foster. 'Two of them are bent as ninepence and the others don't care. Do you?'

'I'd very much like to know where my aunt is,' said Penelope.

'Me too,' I added. 'I'd also like to see that notebook.'

'Neither of which we can help you with,' Foster said. 'Tell you what, give us half an hour before you call the police. Or we'll come back and shoot you.'

'Fair enough,' said Hodge or Hodges.

There was a sound outside. A car.

'Oh what?' said Piano. 'Who's that then?'

He looked at me. 'No idea,' I said.

Everyone else shook their head. We were clearly keen to help.

'Out the back,' said Foster. He and Piano left the room.

'Don't follow us,' he added.

We sat in the front room in silence and listened as the car came up the drive.

'He's left the envelope on the table,' said Hodge or Hodges.

A second later, we all reached for it, like it was the last snack in the bowl. I got to it first. I just had time to slip it into my wallet when the front door opened, Foster said something and then there was a shot, and a thump as of someone falling to the floor.

Penelope ran to the door. I followed. She flung the door open. On the floor was Foster, clutching his leg, which was bleeding. Piano stood beside him, tense. In front of them stood a man holding a pistol.

'Armstrong?' I said.

'Hello, Bread,' said Roger Armstrong, putting the gun away. 'Hello, Penelope,' he added.

Penelope just stared at him.

'Greg?' she said.

Part Three

'I was the only one doing Lowrys at first and now everybody is doing them badly. This is what kills me. The one I did the other day was a lovely Lowry. They are not knocked up in two hours.'
  – David Henty, forger

CHAPTER SEVEN

'And death, for those who live on, is the ending of a chapter rather than the end of the book.'

– John Peel, *Margrave of the Marshes*

'Greg?' I said, '*Greg?*'

'Greg,' said Armstrong. He took Penelope's hand. She jerked it out of his grip again.

'Nice,' he said. 'Come on, let's go back into the front room.'

I looked down. Piano had made a tourniquet from a large pocket handkerchief and was applying it to Foster's leg.

'It's a flesh wound,' said Armstrong. 'Get up and get in there.'

Piano propped Foster up and they made their way into the room. Penelope and I followed. She looked as confused as I was, which was very confused.

Armstrong came into the room after us and closed the door. Hodge and Daventry were already on their feet.

'Hodges, Daventry,' said Armstrong. 'Good work. Wait, no, you lost the notebook.'

'Do you know each other?' I said.

Armstrong turned to me.

'Yes, we know each other, Bread. How slow are you, exactly? And yes, Penelope, my name is Roger. Do I even look like a Greg?'

'You look like a prick,' said Penelope, firmly.

'He is a prick,' I said. I remembered something. 'He takes selfies when he's driving.'

'That is what a prick would do,' said Penelope. 'But I was thinking of other, more prickish things.'

'Yes, I suppose you were,' I said. 'Sorry.'

Penelope stared at Armstrong, or Greg. 'I literally don't know you,' she said.

'No, I suppose you don't,' said Armstrong. 'Oh well, thanks for the sex.'

Penelope turned away in silence.

159

'I don't wish to get shot,' said Piano, 'but what is going on?'

Armstrong sighed.

'I suppose an explanation would fill some time.'

He took a glass of whisky from beside the music centre.

'Jesus, is that still here?' he said. 'I thought my mother would have taken that to a charity shop years ago.'

'Your *mother*?' I said.

'Is there an echo in here?' said Armstrong. 'Yes, there is, and its name is Bread.'

'This is your parents' house,' said Penelope.

'Yes,' said Armstrong, 'although as my father is dead and my mother is in a care home, I suppose to all intents and purposes it is my house. And if you'd met my mother you'd know she'd never have bought that.'

He indicated the Lenkiewicz, an odd mixture of admiration and disgust in his voice.

'That's yours?' I said. 'I thought you hated Lenkiewicz.'

'I do and I don't,' said Armstrong. 'I hate the chocolate–box colours and the melodramatic shadows like he's shouting at you "look what a proper painter I am". But I admire the honesty. This may be mad bollocks, he's saying, but it's mad bollocks from the soul. The other thing I like about Lenkiewicz,' Armstrong added, 'is that he faked his own death. Went to stay with Lord Eliot for a bit and pretended he was deceased. Just to see what it was like. That I do like.'

Something caught Armstrong's eye. It was the tape player.

'This old thing,' he said. 'Good God, there's a cassette in it.'

He pressed play and the tape wobbled into the guitar introduction to 'Wish You Were Here' by Pink Floyd.

'Not one of mother's, I think,' he said. 'Bread, have you been playing your crap?'

I said nothing. I quite liked Pink Floyd.

'Oh well,' said Armstrong. He turned the tape off. 'Where do I begin?' he went on.

He appeared to be considering his options. Then suddenly he reached into his pocket and brought out a small rectangular object.

'The notebook!' said Mary Daventry. 'You took it.'

'Yes,' said Armstrong. 'I took it.'

'What for?' said Hodge. 'You knew we'd find it in the house and we'd bring it to you. That's why you hired us.'

Armstrong looked at me and Penelope.

'Yes,' he said wearily, 'they're working for me. Two out–of–work actors.'

'Stuntman,' said Hodges.

'Whatever,' said Armstrong. 'And no, that's not why I hired you. I didn't need you to bring me the notebook. I knew where it was from the start. From the day Penelope's aunt wrote to me about it. Yes,' he said to Penelope, 'I know your aunt.'

Penelope's face was taut with fury.

'Where is she?' she said.

'She's safe,' said Armstrong. 'I was going to kill her, but she doesn't know anything so what's the point?'

'Where is she?' Penelope said again.

'She's probably home by now,' Armstrong said. 'I let her go on the way here. She was a bit upset about the gag and the cuffs, but I'm sure a cup of tea and a hot bath will sort her out. Tough old bird.'

Penelope lunged at Armstrong. He grabbed her wrists and threw her back. I caught her.

'You piece of shit,' she hissed at Armstrong. 'You trapped me. All for this.'

'I suppose so,' Armstrong said. 'It was very pleasant trapping you, but it was necessary.'

'What was necessary?' I said.

'Yes,' said Piano, 'I'm not following this at all.'

'You're a common thief, I'm not surprised,' said Armstrong. 'But Bread, you're a subtle man. A man of layers. I'm sure you can work it out.'

I thought for a moment.

'You pretended to be this... Greg... character to trick Penelope into having an affair with you,' I said slowly.

'Yes,' said Armstrong. 'Now tell me why.'

'I don't know why,' I said. 'To get to Cora Vanstone?'

'I had already got to Cora Vanstone,' said Armstrong. 'The moment she wrote to me about the notebook I knew she had something of value to me. So I went down to Budleigh to talk to her about it. And that was where I met Penelope.'

'You didn't tell me she'd written to you,' said Penelope.

'I didn't tell you my name, why would I tell you anything?' said Armstrong. 'I wanted to cover my back if something went wrong. So I told Penelope and her aunt that I was Greg Chalmers, which is the name of a former colleague, so if things did go tits up, nothing could be traced to me.'

'And then you invited me for a drink.'

'And then I invited you for a drink,' said Armstrong. 'And I seduced you.'

'Lovely turn of phrase,' said Piano.

'I needed someone like Penelope,' said Armstrong, 'Someone I could manipulate. Someone I thought would appeal to an oik like Bread. He likes classy ladies, don't you Bread? Bit of posh totty?'

'Shut up, Armstrong,' I said.

'Why? What are you going to do? Shoot me?'

I said nothing.

'Seems a lot of fuss to me,' said Piano. 'Why not just nick the notebook? I presume that was the idea. Nick it and flog it on the side.'

'This?' said Armstrong. He snorted. 'This is worth nothing.'

'What?' said Piano. Foster looked startled too.

'Next to nothing,' said Armstrong. 'Maybe twenty thousand pounds.'

'But it's a JM Barrie manuscript,' I said.

'It might be,' said Armstrong. 'And if it is, so what? Even with the *Peter Pan* business, it wouldn't realise more than twenty-five thousand at auction. It's not valueless, and it's historically interesting, but your idiot friend is right. It's not worth all this fuss.'

'Twenty-five grand,' said Piano disbelievingly. 'I'm really glad we didn't kill anyone.'

'Nice to know you've got principles as well as guns,' said Penelope. She was really miffed right now.

'Guns are for the look of the thing mostly,' said Piano. 'Shooting people is amazingly messy. Look at the Yanks. Look at him,' he added, indicating Foster, who was clearly in pain. 'Can we go?' he said to Armstrong.

'What?' Armstrong replied.

'We don't want any trouble, and we can't go to the police,' said Piano. 'Also he needs a doctor. So can we go?'

'No,' said Armstrong. 'Sit over there while I decide what to do with you.'

'Bastard,' said Piano, and carefully moved himself and Foster to the settee.

'And don't bleed on that,' said Armstrong, 'My mother will have my guts for garters.'

'What about us?' said Hodges or Hodge.

'Yes, good point,' said Armstrong. 'But it's hard to trust people, isn't it? And you have proved quite good at deceiving people.'

'You were paying us to deceive people!' said Mary Daventry.

'True,' said Armstrong vaguely. 'Sit over there, anyway.'

Now we were all lined up.

'What now?' said Penelope, sullenly.

'No idea,' said Armstrong. He sniffed a glass of whisky. He examined his gun. He crossed to the tape player and pressed play.

'And that was Suicide, the last from Thin Lizzy tonight, from their 1973 session –'

'Jesus,' said Armstrong, wincing. He snapped the tape machine open and threw me the tape. I caught it and put it in my pocket.

'Can I ask,' said Penelope, after some time had elapsed, 'what we are doing here?'

'We're waiting,' said Armstrong. 'I could fill in the time by telling you what I'm doing here, and why I'm doing it – and,' he added, pointedly, 'I could tell you a few home truths about your man Bread here. But I can do all that later. In the meantime, let's just sit here and wait.'

'I need the toilet,' said Hodges.

'I don't care,' said Armstrong.

A few minutes passed. Armstrong spent the time flicking through the notebook.

'I'd better hang on to this,' he said. 'Maybe get it verified by a real expert.'

I said nothing. Armstrong turned a page.

'Oh,' he said. 'There's a page missing.' He looked at me. I managed to avoid patting my jacket pocket. Armstrong was about to come over when the doorbell rang.

'We'll sort this in a moment, Bread,' he said.

He turned round and called out. 'It's open!'

Lily George walked in, and Armstrong got up and kissed her.

'How was your journey, darling?' he said.

Lily made the sour face that I remembered from our meeting over the Rawley Venus.

'Awful roads, awful people,' she said. She looked around the room. She stared at Penelope.

'So you're the mark,' she said. 'Better looking than I thought you'd be.'

'I wish I could say the same,' said Penelope. Lily's face went, if possible, even more sour. 'Because I have no idea who you are,' Penelope added, sweetly.

'Cat fight,' said Armstrong. 'Marvellous. Now, Lily, you get yourself a drink while we wait for Bread to say something incredibly predictable.'

I felt I might as well. 'I thought she was dead,' I said to Armstrong. 'Murdered.'

'Good work,' said Armstrong. 'No, that was just some silly old cleaner or someone. We needed a body, you see. Lily is fine and dandy, and all ready to go.'

'Almost,' said Lily. 'I'm just going to get some boat clothes from upstairs and then I'm set.'

'Excellent,' said Armstrong. 'That should give me just enough time to tell these people about Bear Family.'

'What?' I said.

'I'm sorry to miss it,' said Lily, and she left the room.

'The bear family?' Hodge said.

'Shut up now,' said Armstrong. 'What I'm going to tell you is – well, I suppose it's the starting point.'

'For what?' Penelope said.

'Everything,' said Armstrong.

'It must have been four or five years ago,' said Armstrong, after he'd made himself comfortable in a large wing-backed chair from which he could see, and if necessary shoot, us all. 'I was reading an article in some magazine or other about – you'll know this, Bread – heritage record labels.'

I nodded. It seemed the thing to do.

'I'm not really a pop fan,' Armstrong continued, 'but it was an interesting business model. It would appear that there's a lot of money to be made packaging up old music and selling it to people who want a bit of – what's the word? Authenticity. Quite right too. I'm all for a bit of authenticity. That's why I work for an auction house. Antiques. Truth and beauty. That sort of thing. People want to own something beautiful, or something old, and more often than not' – and he waved his gun at a large Dresden vase on a nearby table – 'those two things are the same.'

'Is this a long story?' said Penelope.

'Rude,' said Armstrong. 'So anyway, this article was all about a record label in Germany called Bear Family. And what they do is track down rare old recordings by blues singers and whatnot, clean them up, repackage them and sell them to the sort of people who like that sort of thing. All completely fine and above board. Except that halfway down the page, there was a bit where they interviewed the man who does their artwork, and he said an extraordinary thing.'

Armstrong reached into his pocket and, to my surprise, pulled out a torn and folded bit of paper.

'Kept it,' he explained. 'You can see it meant a lot to me. Changed my life, even.'

He unfolded the paper and began to read.

'When I retouch photographs' – this is the art director talking – 'When I retouch photographs the greatest challenge is to not look like a digital result. There were times when I restored an old photo from 1928 that looked like it had been in some cowboy's backpack for 20 years but it just looked too clean! So I took little scratches and distortions from the original and put them in *on the edges so the whole thing looked like an old photo again but like an old photo fresh from the photographer's shop on Main Street.'*

He looked at us.

'Nothing?' he said.

'I don't get it,' said Hodges.

'I am surrounded by philistines,' Armstrong said. 'Bread? Any inkling at all?'

'The art director is faking it,' I said. 'He's taking something that's real and authentic – the old, original photographs – and he's making them look, not like they did when they were taken, but like he imagines they ought to look. A more commercially acceptable version of reality. It's a kind of forgery.'

'And you'd know all about that,' said Armstrong. 'But yes, you're right. And the more I thought about this, the more it niggled at me. I started to do some research.'

'Into forgery?' I asked.

'Into forgery,' said Armstrong. 'And do you know what I found out? That nobody cares. Nobody gives a fig if an objet d'art or an antique is the real thing or not. So long as it can be sold, who cares if it's a fake? That is the attitude of my profession.'

'I think you're being a bit simplistic,' I said.

'I don't care what you think,' said Armstrong. 'The point is, I suddenly realised that I had been wasting my life. Running up and down the country, examining antiques and checking them out to see if they were *real* or not. What a pointless exercise. The buyers don't care, sellers don't care. Nobody cares.'

'I thought you could get into trouble for selling fakes,' said Hodge.

'Oh you can,' said Armstrong. 'Because people have to be made examples of, don't they? But what happens to the forgers when they're released? They carry on doing the same thing, only they call themselves copyists. They get their own TV shows. They become *experts*. Whereas people like me – we're the mugs. Slogging away for peanuts, watching crooks get rich while we hold their hands and tell them the difference between Louis Quinze and Louis bloody Armstrong.'

He refolded the paper again, put it back in his pocket.

'Well, I'd had enough. I saw everyone else being completely unscrupulous and nobody, as I say, giving a monkey's, so I thought –'

'You thought you'd join in,' said Penelope. 'Another snout at the trough.'

'Yes,' said Armstrong. 'Harsh choice of words but fair.'

Lily came back into the room. Improbably, she was wearing oilskin trousers. She was carrying a second pair, which she threw to Armstrong.

'And so,' said Armstrong, 'I was clear in my mind about what I wanted to do. I was going to get my hands dirty. I was going to make some money. I was going to be somewhat sloppy about provenance and fudge like crazy. The only question was how.'

'And then,' he said, looking lovingly at her, 'I met lily.'

'Put your trousers on,' said Lily, clearly not the romantic sort. 'The tide's up.'

'Lily was perfect,' said Armstrong, obeying her. 'Beautiful, intelligent and, almost as important, with access to an awful lot of antiques.'

'The Rawley Collection,' I said.

'Quite,' said Armstrong. 'The plan was simple. Lily would persuade the board of the Rawley Collection that some items needed to be valued for future sale. She'd earmark a few candidates from the dodgy shelf –'

'The what?' said Penelope.

'The dodgy shelf,' said Armstrong. 'Every great collection has one, I expect. In the Rawley's case it's literally a shelf of pieces which don't quite feel right. Not exactly iffy, but not properly authenticated.'

'And your plan was to get these pieces authenticated, and then sell them on,' I said. 'But how do you make money from that? You'd just get commission.'

'Smart boy,' said Lily.

'That wasn't our plan at all,' said Armstrong. 'As I was saying before I was so rudely interrupted, our plan was to get a few items from the dodgy shelf together and then chuck in a couple of ringers. Real pieces, pieces with fairly solid history. And then get them... de-authenticated.'

'I'm not with you,' said Hodges. 'How do you de-authenticate something?'

I saw it then.

'You get some idiot in who thinks he's spotted a fake,' I said. 'Some cocky, overconfident fool who reckons they've spotted a clue.'

'Exactly,' said Armstrong. 'You, in other words.'

'The Rawley Vulcan,' I explained to Penelope. 'I saw a couple of things that didn't feel right.'

'I can't believe it was so easy,' said Armstrong. 'All we did was scratch a couple of words on the base and those silly hammers on the apron.'

'My idea,' said Lily. 'He didn't like the idea of defacing a work of art, but I told him we could get the marks off again.'

'And so Bread came down and he said the Vulcan was a fake, and I pretended to get terribly upset, and Lily told the board what had happened, and they asked her to quietly dispose of it,' said Armstrong.

'They even told me they didn't want to know what I did with it,' said Lily, cheerfully.

'And that's what we've been doing ever since,' Armstrong said. 'Going round the country, looking at people's nice things and telling them that they're not worth anything. We're a kind of *Antiques Roadshow* in reverse. And we couldn't do it without Bread.'

He smiled at me. It wasn't a pleasant smile.

'I never worked it out, Bread,' said Armstrong, 'this whole Antiques Whisperer thing – do you believe it yourself or is it a total con? Because it was very effective.'

I continued to say nothing.

'I mean, yes, you had some successes. The Lawrence thing. Pring's hired you on the basis of that. Very impressive. And a couple of others. But mostly I imagine you're like one of those awful mediums. A few lucky guesses and the odd inspired moment and everyone forgets the flops. Is that it, Bread? Am I warm?'

'Does it matter?' I said, finally. Penelope wasn't even looking in my direction now.

'Not really,' said Armstrong, his point made. 'We used you, and your fantastic ability to spot obvious fakes at fifty paces, and I'm terribly sorry and all that, but boo hoo.'

'You can't keep doing this for ever,' said Penelope. 'You'll get caught.'

'Oh, I know,' said Lily. 'Which is why we're stopping.'

'Tonight,' said Armstrong. 'It's a tough habit to break, because it's so lucrative. But habits are bad. So we're off. America.'

'Might even start again,' said Lily.

'Got new identities, have you?' said Piano.

'The lot,' Armstrong said. 'One thing about making friends with forgers, getting new passports is a doddle. Although you do have to check them for spelling mistakes.'

'It's true,' I told Penelope, unable to stop myself. 'A forger called David Henty was caught when he made hundreds of passports with the words "Britannic" and "Majesty" spelled wrong.'

'You seem to know a lot about forgery,' said Penelope. She sounded even less happy.

'Picking up on my subtle hints, are you?' said Armstrong. 'Slowly realising that your man Bread isn't all he's cracked up to be?'

Penelope looked him straight in the eye.

'Whatever he is, he's better than you.'

'Even if he's a liar?' said Lily. 'Three years open prison, did he mention that? White–collar crime, document fraud?'

She leant down and looked Penelope in the eye.

'New life under a new name?' she said. 'Did that come up between the sheets?'

'They didn't,' said Armstrong.

'They did,' said Lily. 'I can always tell.'

'Goodness,' said Armstrong. He stared at Penelope.

'You didn't really think he was called Charlie *Bread*, did you?'

Penelope ignored him.

'They're not lying, are they?' she said.

I looked down at the floor.

'Answer me, please,' said Penelope.

I didn't look her in the eye as I said, 'No. They're not lying.'

'Who are you then?' Penelope said. 'Actually, don't tell me. I don't care.'

'And there we have it,' said Armstrong. 'Everything in its right place. Now come along everyone, we've got to go.'

'Are we taking all of them?' said Lily.

'Just to the meeting point,' Armstrong said. 'Except these two.'

He indicated Piano and the almost-unconscious Foster.

'They're common criminals. They're not going to say anything. Are you?' he asked.

'Glad to be shot of you,' said Piano. 'No pun intended.'

'Quite,' said Armstrong. 'Besides, who knows? Maybe our paths will cross again.'

'Hope not,' said Piano.

Armstrong smiled a thin-lipped smile and turned to Lily.

'Come on,' he said, 'let's get the cattle out of here.'

We were ushered, Penelope and I, Hodges and Daventry, out of the house at gunpoint. The rain was coming down heavily now as we were made to walk, first across a large muddy field, and then down a set of steep and winding stone steps, slippery and uneven, to a tiny jetty, tied to which was a cabin cruiser just about big enough to take five people.

The wind was too loud to permit conversation, which was just as well. Penelope wasn't speaking to me, Mary Daventry had lapsed into confused silence some time ago, and Hodges was mostly concerned that she didn't lose her footing. I wondered what their relationship had been before all this.

I looked back at the house. I could see light spilling out from where the front door was still open. Piano or whatever his real name was must have been standing outside waiting for the ambulance. Out here it could take a while to get to the house and I found myself, oddly, hoping it would get there soon.

There was a shout and I turned to see Penelope and the others being shoved onto the boat as it swayed and lurched in the heavy tide.

'Get on, Bread,' shouted Armstrong. 'We want your company most of all.' And he pushed me onto the boat. The deck was slippery and I nearly went over.

I made to go below but immediately realised that there was no 'below'. The wheelhouse aside, there was no cover on the boat at all, and everyone save the person driving it (I suspected this was the wrong word) was forced to hold on to the brass rail running round the side of the boat for safety.

'Where are we going?' said Penelope to Lily.

'Somewhere we won't be interrupted,' she replied.

The seas were not pleasant. There was a powerful headwind to fight against, and great gouts of salt water flew at us constantly. The boat itself went up and down the waves with an alarming lack of surefootedness and there seemed to be a lot of rocks everywhere.

'It's time, I think,' Armstrong called to Lily.

'You should have done it back at the house!' she replied.

'I don't think my mother would have been very happy,' shouted Armstrong, and without any warning, he charged at Mary Daventry, who screamed and immediately went backwards over the side of the boat. Without a word, Hodges followed her into the waves.

'I thought he might be trouble,' shouted Armstrong. 'Oh well, bit of a bonus.'

'Why did you do that?' Penelope screamed. 'You bastard!'

'Too many cooks,' Armstrong replied. 'Or something. It's funny, isn't it,' he bellowed, 'I don't mind letting a pair of thieves go. But actors – can't trust them to keep their mouths shut.'

He went to talk to the driver. Penelope put her hands over her face. I went to put my arms around her, but she pushed me away.

'This is your fault,' she said.

I couldn't disagree. I went to the side, but there was no sign of life in the waves. I didn't think there would be. And then I saw a light, blinking in the darkness.

'We're heading towards a lighthouse!' I told Penelope.

She didn't even look up.

Killigrew Rock isn't the most westerly point in the British Isles, but it might as well be. After Killigrew, there's nothing but America, and that's a few thousand miles away. But it's the last thing you see as you cross the Atlantic and it's an impressive sight. A very large, flat-topped rock rising out of the sea like the top half of a rook in chess, with a similarly flat-topped lighthouse, white and squat with a helicopter landing pad on the roof.

Ropes and chains led from an almost sheltered mooring point to the lighthouse door and, once we'd tied up, we managed to make our way across the rock. I won't say it wasn't an entirely terrifying walk, because it was. More than once I lost my footing and had to scrabble along the rope to regain it.

Armstrong watched as the boat headed back into the waves and then motioned for us to go inside the lighthouse, where total silence prevailed. He indicated to Penelope and me that we should start climbing the stairs. I wondered if he was planning to push us off the top, then reflected that he could have easily done to us what he did to Hodges and Daventry in the boat, and headed on up.

At the top of the stairs was an open doorway. We went through it to something that resembled a small common room or rest area. Presumably whoever visited this lighthouse was meant to relax here in between fixing the big light or whatever it is people do when they're sent to automated lighthouses. Either way, it was spartan but comfortable, with a large sofa, a TV, radio and even – I was amused despite myself – a large 1980s-style ghetto blaster.

'Oh my,' said Armstrong, seeing my expression, 'a Brixton briefcase. How quaint. Probably worth a bit to the right hipster, I shouldn't be surprised.'

Lily pushed Penelope onto the sofa.

'What's this?' she said. She reached under Penelope's coat and, after a slight struggle, came out with my dad's gun.

'Good Lord,' said Armstrong. 'Well, that makes life easier. Hoist with their own petard.'

'I can't believe you didn't search them,' Lily said.

'Jesus,' said Armstrong, irritated. 'I'll do it now.'

Lily patted Penelope down and Armstrong went through my pockets. There was nothing of interest to him, I could tell, except the cassette, which he set aside with unusual care.

'That'll come in handy for your confession,' he said.

I was tired of saying things like 'what confession?' and 'what are you talking about?' all the time, so I said nothing. Instead I watched in some confusion as Armstrong opened the ghetto blaster and put the cassette in.

Penelope brushed Lily away from her and went over to what I supposed was a porthole (I wasn't really up on lighthouse lore). The beam continued to sweep around us, illuminating huge rolling slabs of grey.

'Why,' she said, 'are we in a lighthouse?'

'Because we wanted to be as far away from the mainland as possible,' said Armstrong. 'Because we need a bit of peace and quiet. Because this is the final step for all of us, some more than others.'

I have to say, I didn't like that last remark at all.

'And,' said Armstrong, 'because you can land a helicopter on the roof of this thing.'

'Seems reasonable,' said Penelope. 'I'm still not sure why we're here.' She sounded remarkably calm in the circumstances and I could only suppose this was firstly because she'd decided that I was a useless let–down and secondly because terrifying situations concentrate the mind wonderfully.

'People like you never do work it out,' said Lily. 'Never taking control. Never acting, always reacting. Always floating around on the lower rungs.'

'Can you float around on rungs?' said Penelope.

'Shut up,' said Lily, thereby making it one–nil to Penelope. She turned to Armstrong. 'How long now?' she said.

'Not long,' Armstrong replied, looking at his watch. 'I suppose we'd better get on with it. Shall I do the explanation or cut to the chase?'

'God, cut to the chase,' said Lily. 'Give us all a break.'

Armstrong looked angry then, and I suspected that his relationship with Lily might not be going too well. I imagined that all the theft and murder might have created a bit of a strain between them.

'Oh but I think they deserve an explanation,' he said, and I could see Lily's brow actually furrow. Now I was wondering if their relationship would survive the helicopter escape, never mind a new life in America.

'Fine,' said Lily, 'I'll go and do something useful.'

She left the room. Armstrong shrugged.

'It's the stress,' he said. 'Now, where were we?'

'You were going to do the explanation,' I said.

'Of course,' said Armstrong. He looked at his watch.

'Shit,' he said. 'Right, I'll keep this brief.'

'Must you?' said Penelope, who like me had a feeling where this might be going.

'You see, everything is all tied up,' said Armstrong. 'All the witnesses are gone – except Piano and Foster, and they're hardly going to tell anyone what happened – which leaves you, and you.'

'So why not dump us in the sea?' I said.

' Lily was all for it,' said Armstrong. 'She's not a warm woman. But I said no, Bread. I said, the thing is, Lily, I loathe this man. I hate everything he stands for, from his cheap suit to his stupid music. His fake name – oh yes, when I found out you were starting a new life I wasn't surprised. People like you, Bread, always think they can just rip up the parchment and start again.'

'That's what you're doing,' Penelope pointed out.

'I have to, though,' said Armstrong. 'Bread didn't. All he had to do was apologise to the people he'd defrauded and do some penance and then he'd be forgiven. But Bread's too much of a coward for that. He just goes round pretending he can magically tell what's real and what's not real, and suckers fall for it.'

'Get to the point, please,' I said.

'Sorry, Bread, bit close to the bone, am I?' Armstrong said. 'Very well. Now we come to it. You see, Lily and I have made our omelette, as it were, and we've cracked a lot of eggs. We've left a trail and it leads, if not exactly to us, then to the rough vicinity of Pring's. Emails, receipts, letters, all manner of things which point to rather dubious deals. So it's time for us to tidy up.'

'I wonder how you're going to do that,' said Penelope, with a dead tone in her voice.

'I'm sure you've guessed,' said Armstrong. 'Pin it on old Charlie here. He'll record a confession on this conveniently located tape machine,' – Armstrong indicated the ghetto blaster with a wave of his gun – 'and then he'll kill himself. All neat and tidy. Except for his brains being all over the shop, obviously.'

'He's not going to record a confession,' Penelope said, looking disdainfully at me.

'He is,' said Armstrong. 'And you know why, don't you, Bread?'

'Yes,' I said. 'Because if I don't, you'll kill Penelope.'

'Smart fellow,' said Armstrong. 'You see, Penelope, I have no reason to off you. You're the one who's left behind to radio the mainland and so forth. Call the cops and the coastguard.'

'What's to stop me calling the police on you?' said Penelope. I noticed she had so far failed to express any concerns about the whole me-blowing-my-brains-out aspect of the plan.

'Humiliation,' said Armstrong. 'Having to go home and admit to everyone you know – and the press, and the TV news – that you were so desperate and lonely that you fell for everything. That I fooled you, and Bread fooled you, and that you're a trusting idiot. You'll be the laughing stock of the world, not just your village.'

Penelope looked thoughtful.

'How do you know he'll do it?' she said.

'He won't, he's a coward,' said Armstrong. 'So I'll put the gun in his mouth and I'll pull the trigger.'

'I am still here, you know,' I said.

'Not for long, though,' said Armstrong.

Lily appeared in the doorway.

'Haven't you done it yet?' she said. 'Too busy talking, I expect. Men,' she said to Penelope. 'They're always saying we're the ones who talk too much but get them on their favourite topic...'

'You've forgotten something,' I said.

'Have we now?' said Armstrong.

'I've still got the scrap of paper from the notebook.'

'Oh, who cares?' said Lily. 'We can get it off your corpse later.'

'Might be a bit bloody,' I pointed out. 'Also it's in my wallet. Might get a bullet through it.'

Penelope had the decency to look ill.

'How helpful,' said Armstrong.

He reached into my jacket and removed my wallet. He opened the wallet and took out the envelope. He was about to put it in his pocket when I said: 'Aren't you going to check it's there?'

'Why?' said Armstrong. A look crossed his face, as though he thought something might be awry.

'It's part of a rare document,' I said. 'Better make sure it's all right.'

'Playing for time, are we?' said Armstrong. 'Very well then.'

He opened the envelope and removed the scrap of paper.

'What's this?' he said.

'What's going on?' said Lily.

'This isn't from the notebook,' said Armstrong. 'What the hell is this?'

He unfolded it and began to read it out loud.

'When we trod this land, we walk for one reason…'

Lily said, 'Please just shoot him.'

'When we trod this land, we walk for one reason…' I said, *'The reason is to try to help another man to think for himself. The music of our hearts is roots music: music which recalls history…'*

I moved towards Armstrong, still talking. He was uncertain, wondering what to do.

'Because without the knowledge of your history, you cannot determine your destiny,' I said, looking him in the eye, *'The music about the present, because if you are not conscious of the present, you are like a cabbage in this society.'*

'Seriously,' said Lily, 'give me the gun, I'll do it.'

'Music which tells about the future,' I said, *'And the judgement which is to come.'*

'What?' said Armstrong. I was right in his face now. He almost stumbled backwards. Then he righted himself. He stuck the gun in my eye.

'What the hell was that about?' he hissed.

'Misty in Roots,' I said. *'Live at the Counter Eurovision 79.* It was one of John Peel's favourite albums.'

'This is just stalling,' said Lily. 'Can we get this done, please?'

Armstrong looked at me, trying to work out what was going on. Then, deciding he didn't care, he pulled the gun away.

'Where's the real scrap of paper?' he said.

'In the glove compartment of the Jag,' I said.

'We can get that later then,' said Armstrong. 'Give me the tape,' he said to Lily. Lily picked up my cassette from the table and Armstrong slotted it into the ghetto blaster. He pressed record. Nothing happened. He pressed it again.

'There's something wrong with it,' he said.

'You need to replace the tabs,' I said.

'Shut up,' said Armstrong. He jabbed at it again.

'Now you're fast forwarding,' I said.

'Shut *up*,' said Armstrong and jabbed at it again. Suddenly the tape began to play. John Peel's voice, loud and amplified.

'Now for those who missed last week's programmes,' said Peel, *'I'm currently working my way through my personal top sixty of 1977.'*

'Turn it off, you idiot,' said Lily.

'Wait,' I said, 'What did he just say?'

'I realise this is blindingly irrelevant, but it does afford me some innocent pleasure,' Peel said, *'Here's number 31.'*

And then 'Love Story' by The Lurkers came on, number 31 in the 1977 Festive Sixty – because did I mention there were sixty songs in it, not fifty? – the chart that was the Holy Grail for Peel fans, the long-lost show that nobody could find, but was playing here, now, on this machine.

The rough punk blasted through the room.

'Jesus Christ!' shouted Lily, goaded beyond endurance. She reached for the tape machine.

'Just leave it to me,' shouted Armstrong. He hit stop, and as he did so, I punched him in the eye. Armstrong shouted in pain, and came at me with the gun, trying to hit my face.

'Don't hit him with a loaded gun!' shouted Lily. 'You might shoot me!'

'Stop fucking telling me what to do!' shouted Armstrong. He lunged for my head with the gun. The gun missed and connected with the wall. Just as Lily had predicted, it went off, and a bullet narrowly missed me.

I punched Armstrong in the face. He dropped the gun and it skittered across the floor. Lily leapt at me. I tried to get out of the way, but too late. She had me on the ground and was punching me in the head with both fists, shouting something I couldn't hear because of the incessant pummelling. I rolled over and tried to get her off my back, but she just leapt up and started kicking me.

Then suddenly Lily was off balance and staggering to one side. Penelope had grabbed her and pulled her off. With a shove, Lily sent Penelope flying.

'No!' I shouted and tried to get to my feet. I felt a foot press down on my chest. I looked up and Armstrong was standing over me with his gun.

'Let's do this,' he said.

'Let her go,' I said. 'Kill me, I don't care.'

'Yes you do,' said Armstrong. 'That's the best bit. The question is, who do I kill first?'

I couldn't speak.

'Best close your eyes,' Armstrong said.

I stared up at him. I wanted him to remember me, remember the rage and the contempt for him.

'Have it your own way,' he said, and aimed the gun at my face.

There was a click.

'That's odd,' I said. 'Your gun doesn't have a safety catch.'

Lily turned. Penelope was standing behind her and Armstrong with my dad's pistol.

'I thought you took the bullets out,' said Armstrong to Lily.

'She put them back when I distracted you with the Misty in Roots speech,' I said.

'Will you please stop explaining everything?' said Penelope.

'Sorry,' I said.

'Untie him,' Penelope told Lily. A few seconds later, I was free and Lily and Armstrong were in the corner, our guns pointing at them.

It was a lot nicer that way, I must say.

Penelope and I sat at the other end of the room.

'What are we doing?' she said.

'Waiting for the helicopter,' I said.

'Will they come down here?'

'Unlikely. Once they realise Armstrong and Lily aren't going to make the rendezvous, they'll bugger off again. Which is better for us.'

'I suppose so. What are we going to do then?'

'Radio the mainland for someone to come and get us.'

Penelope looked at me.

'Is that someone expecting a call?'

I realised the game was up.

'Yes,' I said. 'I mean, maybe not right this minute, and if things went wrong, then not expecting a call, but yes.'

'Who are you?' said Penelope.

'Robert,' I said. 'Robert Smith.'

She narrowed her eyes. 'That's a singer's name.'

'I know,' I said. 'Oddly, the fact that I have the same name as the lead singer of The Cure has been brought to my attention over the years.'

'Is that why you changed it?'

'No,' I said. 'I changed it for… work reasons. I wanted a name that sounded a bit wrong. A name that someone like Roger Armstrong would think looked a bit iffy. Which would encourage him in his hopefully already strong suspicions.'

'I'm not entirely with you,' Penelope said.

'I wanted Armstrong to suspect me,' I said. 'With the name and the whole Antiques Whisperer thing. I wanted him to smell a rat concerning me. So he'd do some digging, and find out that I had a criminal record.'

'Do you have a criminal record?'

'No. Not a real one. Just one planted in the official record for Armstrong to find.'

'But why?'

'So I'd think he wasn't kosher,' said Armstrong wearily. 'So I'd be tempted into using a person who I thought was a conman and a cheat for my own ends.'

'I knew Armstrong would have trusted one of his own,' I said. 'Old school tie and that. I had to be his idea of scum – a comprehensive–educated lowlife who he'd have no hesitation in dumping on.'

'You are scum,' said Lily.

'I didn't bargain on all of this,' I said to Penelope. 'Meeting you, and Lily vanishing and reappearing, and Piano and Foster following me. But I had to flush Armstrong out. That's why Pring's hired me.'

'Pring's?' said Armstrong disbelievingly.

'Oh,' I said, 'is there an echo in here? Yes, Pring's. They found me online – I worked for the Art and Antiques bit of the Fraud Squad – and they persuaded me to freelance for them. The A and A has zero resources anyway, so it worked out better that way. They were onto someone diddling them, but they couldn't prove it.'

'You're telling me that you're an undercover cop?' said Penelope in disbelief.

'I'm sorry,' I said. 'I had to lie to you. But I didn't... everything I felt was real.'

'What does he mean?' said Lily.

'He means he slept with her using a false name, the disgusting cad,' said Armstrong.

'I lied about my job and my name,' I said. 'But I – well, I love you, Penelope.'

'Please shoot me,' said Lily.

'Shut up or I'll tape your fat face up,' said Penelope. 'We can talk about that later,' she said to me. 'Finish your story.'

'I couldn't get anything on Armstrong,' I said. 'And the Rawley Vulcan was such a bad fake that if I'd pretended not to spot it, he would have smelled a rat. It was going badly, until he made a mistake.'

'Oh, do tell,' said Armstrong, tetchily.

'The letter and the notebook from Cora Vanstone,' I said. 'She'd been in touch with you, all right. And it was the perfect way to get me reeled in so you could pin everything on me and get away.'

'So what did I do?' sneered Armstrong. 'Because I didn't touch the notebook. I genuinely have no idea if it was written by Barrie or the girl.'

'It wasn't the notebook,' I said. 'It was the letter.'

'What do you mean?' asked Penelope.

'Armstrong got Cora's letter about the notebook over a year ago. But he couldn't just put it in a drawer while he and Lily made their plans. He needed time to set everything in motion. So – he altered it. He changed the date.'

'And I suppose your eagle eyes noted a different ink, did they?' said Armstrong.

'No,' I said. 'Because Cora Vanstone wrote to you on the twenty-ninth of February, 2016. And you changed the date to the following year.'

'So?' said Armstrong.

'You *wanker*,' said Lily, with feeling.

'What?' Armstrong said.

'2016 was a leap year,' said Lily. 'Which is why there was a twenty-ninth of February. And which is why there wasn't a twenty-ninth of February in 2017.'

'Oh fuck,' said Armstrong.

'After that,' I said, 'it was easy. I told Pring's I thought I'd got you, and we set the wheels in motion. But,' I said to Penelope, 'I had no idea that I would meet you. I never intended to use you or involve you.'

'But you shagged her anyway,' said Armstrong.

Penelope opened a drawer and pulled out a roll of gaffer tape. Armstrong fell silent.

'And here we are,' I said. 'Two people are dead – three, including that innocent cleaner – and for what? Money and arrogance.'

'Shh,' said Penelope. 'I think they're here.'

We fell silent as the noise of a helicopter became audible above our heads. We listened for several minutes and then the noise receded.

'They didn't even bother to land,' said Penelope.

'No point,' I said.

Suddenly Armstrong made a bolt for the door. I fired at him and missed. Lily decided to take her chances as well. I raised my gun again but Penelope touched my arm.

'Where are they going to go?' she said.

We went outside in the lashing rain. I could see Armstrong and Lily making their way down the ladder to the jetty. Perhaps they thought they could attract the helicopter's attention somehow. Perhaps they hoped there would be a boat below. I'll never know, because just as they reached ground level, Lily slipped on a rock, careened into Armstrong, and they both went flying, straight over the side of the jetty and into the waves.

They didn't come up again. After a while, Penelope and I went back inside and I radioed the mainland.

CHAPTER EIGHT

Cocklecarrot (roaring): Then what is your name, you oaf?
The Dwarf: Charlie Bread. *(Laughter and jeers)*
Cocklecarrot: Clear the court! This foolery is intolerable. It will ruin my political career.

– Beachcomber, 'The Case of the Red-Headed Dwarfs', part 11

Penelope didn't speak to me on the flight back. She didn't speak to me afterwards either. I had her email address and I sent her my phone number, and I waited, but nothing.

Ivor was happy to get the Jag back in one piece, especially when I paid up the excess time on the rental.

I had a long meeting with the police, who seemed a bit confused by events, but there we go.

Pring's were disappointed that Armstrong and Lily weren't around to account for what they'd sold and what they'd stolen, but even they had to agree that it was all tied up and they said they'd be in touch if they needed me again.

I listened to the Peel tape again, which I'd retrieved before we were picked up from the lighthouse, and confirmed that it was the missing 1977 Festive Fifty, or Sixty. I posted the details on a John Peel fan site and, while people were surprised and grateful that it had been found, there was also a sense of disappointment that the unfindable had now been found. There will be, however, other shows to track down, and the discovery of the Grail shows that anything is possible.

Some time after, I was walking through central London, wondering if newspapers still ran JOBS WANTED ads, when I saw a stocky man pushing a wheelchair along the pavement. He saw me, and tried to cross the road, but I stood in front of them and blocked his escape.

'Hello, Mary,' I said to the woman in the wheelchair. 'Hello, Hodges.'

Mary Daventry said nothing. Hodges grunted.

'I thought you were dead,' I said.

'Hodges saved me,' said Daventry. 'I'll be in this chair for a few months, but he's looking after me.'

'How did you get to shore?' I said.

'Told you,' said Hodges, 'Stuntman.' And with a shove he pushed me out of the way and set off with the chair again.

My dad called.

'Robert?' he said.

'Hi, Dad, how's it going?'

'Fine, thanks. Are you coming down any time soon?'

'I could do. When were you thinking?'

'How about now?'

'What, right now?'

'That would be good.'

'Are you all right, Dad?'

'Just get down here.'

I got the train this time, and a taxi to my dad's. I knocked on the door. A woman answered it. She was about my dad's age, and she looked familiar.

'You're Cora Vanstone,' I said. 'The real one.'

'Come in,' she said, and I followed her into my dad's front room. He was sitting on the settee, but he stood up when she came in. He was always a polite man, my dad.

Dad made us coffee and we all sat down.

'I'm afraid the police took your pistol,' I said to my dad.

'That's all right,' my dad said. 'I'm just glad it all got sorted. And that Cora is all right.'

He patted her hand. She reciprocated, and smiled at him.

'I'm sorry you got involved in all this,' I said to her. 'Are you all right?'

'I've been worse,' said the real Cora. 'And it was nice to learn that your father was concerned about me.'

I reached into my pocket. 'I was going to post this to you,' I said, and gave Cora the notebook.

She opened it. 'The cause of all the trouble,' she said, and smiled. 'I don't suppose you have any idea if it's real or not?'

I took it from her again. 'The handwriting is almost certainly a child's,' I said. 'Which doesn't preclude a child being asked to copy out someone else's words, or that someone was skilled at forging a child's handwriting.'

'So no news is good news,' said my dad.

'There is something, though,' I said. 'At the back, there's a list of titles, as though the writer were trying out ideas...'

But they weren't listening. They were looking at someone over my shoulder. I turned to see Penelope. This time I was the one who stood up.

'Hello – Robert,' she said.

'Penelope,' I responded, wittily.

'I heard you were coming down,' she said. 'I've been staying with Aunt Cora and I thought we could – go for a walk or something.'

'Very underrated, walks,' said my dad.

'Be quiet, you,' said Cora.

Penelope and I went for a walk. It was cold, and she put her arm around me.

'I've been thinking a lot,' she said. 'About what happened, and about you.'

'Have you reached a conclusion?' I said, sounding as much like an idiot as possible.

'Not yet,' she said. 'You lied to me, and that's not good. I mean, I know Greg – Armstrong – was worse, but that's not the point. You didn't trust me, and I don't like that.'

'I'm sorry,' I said.

'Good,' she said. 'I'd be even more annoyed if you weren't sorry.'
She looked at me.

'This is me,' she said. 'This is always me. There isn't anyone else I
can be, or anything else. So I need to know – is this you?'

I took her hand.

'My name is Robert Smith,' I said. 'Like the singer. I called myself
Charlie Bread partly because I needed a new name and partly as a trib-
ute to Beachcomber.'

'I know I'm going to regret this,' said Penelope. 'But who is Beachcomber?'

'He was a very funny writer. I got into him after John Peel mentioned being a fan.'

'I thought Charlie Bread was a pretty silly name.'

'Double bluff. I reckoned if I gave myself a slightly ludicrous name,
people would think it must be real.'

'You're an idiot. And a fool.'

'I know. But that name is done with now. I'm not lying to you any
more, and I never will again.'

Penelope raised an eyebrow.

'Really?' she said.

'Yes,' I said.

'All right,' she said, and grinned. Then she kissed me.

EPILOGUE

It is 1890. A young girl is sitting at a table, her legs tucked under a chair that is slightly too big for her. She is concentrating as she writes in her notebook. She stops writing for a moment, thinks, and, grabbing her pencil firmly, presses it hard into the paper and writes, with a decisiveness that would impress any critic:

'*The Young Visiters, or Mister Salteena's Plan.*'

Her mother comes in.

'Come along now,' she says, kindly. 'It's time for tea.'

Daisy Ashford puts down her pencil, closes her notebook and runs into the dining room.

Postscript

Most of the facts in this book are true. Some are almost true. And a few are not true at all.

JM Barrie is generally reckoned to have altered Sylvia Du Maurier's will to enable him to become her children's guardian. Several people, most notably Winston Churchill, believed him to be the real author of *The Young Visiters.* I am not one of those people.

The Parminter sisters of A La Ronde were devout Christians, and the story of the oaks that could not be felled is one which inspired many Christians in the nineteenth century, but it is, by all accounts, a fabrication. There is more information on this excellent site: http://jsbookreader.blogspot.co.uk/2011/12/oaks-of-la-ronde.html.

Peter Pan continues to be in copyright, thanks to an Act of Parliament that has never been repealed.

The Pet Shop Boys did record a session for John Peel, broadcast on 10 August 2002, but they used the occasion to showcase some songs they'd never committed to vinyl; to my immense regret, they didn't record a new version of their wonderful lost–generation lament, 'Go West'.

Paul Simon did credit the running time of the 45 of 'Fakin' It' as two minutes and seventy-four seconds. John Peel played 'Fakin' It' on his final *Perfumed Garden* show of 14 August 1967. As with all other extracts (barring one exception), the between–song speech is real, and transcribed from actual editions of Peel's shows.

The Rawley Vulcan and the Rawley Collection are entirely fictional, although the sculptor Aleijadinho is not.

Everything about Robert Lenkiewicz is, so far as I know, true.

Everything about Ted Carroll is not true.

Both *The Young Visiters* and its parody *The Young Immigrunts* are marvellous books, and well worth investigating. The section quoted from *The Young Immigrunts* is, in the opinion of many, the funniest piece of writing ever. I have no dispute with this viewpoint.

The 1977 Festive Fifty (or Sixty) has, at the time of writing, still not been found, but it does exist, and thanks to the extensive efforts of tape collectors and the superb John Peel Wiki, no doubt it one day will be.

I am indebted to CM Taylor for his superb development editing and Andrew Chapman for his excellent copy editing, Tara Lee-Platt of TLP Research for expert advice and information concerning the possible value of a JM Barrie manuscript, to Tot Taylor of the Riflemaker Gallery for insider information about the art world's attitude to fakery, and to my dad, Michael Quantick, for encouragement, advice and books.

I researched this book from large chunks of the internet, a lot of John Peel shows and several other books. Some of those books are:

David Cavanagh: *Goodnight and Good Riddance: How 35 Years of John Peel Helped to Shape Modern Life*
Rick Gekoski: *Lost, Stolen or Shredded: Stories of Missing Works of Art and Literature*
Lionel Hampshire: *The Twilight of Otters*
Eric Hobsbawm and Thomas Ranger (editors): *The Invention of Tradition*
Jonathon Keats: *Forged: Why Fakes Are the Great Art of Our Age*
AJB Kiddell: *Fakes and Reproductions in China, Glass and Other Works of Art*
John Peel and Sheila Ravenscroft: *Margrave of the Marshes*
Peter York: *Authenticity is a Con*

All errors, intentional and otherwise, are mine alone.

Patrons

Liz Bailey
Nicholas Baker
Jason Ballinger
Kimberly Bright
Sally Brindle
James Collingwood
Glen Colson
Fiona Cox
Toni Da
Iain Davies
Stephen Davies
John Dexter
Mark Doggart
Barry Featherston
Patrick Fitzgerald
Amro Gebreel
David Gibson
Mark Gillies
Lisa Goldsmith
Georgia Greer
John Guthrie
Kate Hardie
Pamela Hardyment
Simon Harper
Caitlin Harvey
Peter Hobbins
Richard Holmes
Jolyon Holroyd
Marjorie Johns
Stefanie Kudla
Roger Langridge
William Leitch

Scott Longley
Rory Manchee
Fraser McAlpine
Tracy McAteer
Ryan McRostie
Margo Milne
Sarah Morgan
Jim Mortleman
Carlo Navato
Neil Perryman
Alexander Peterhans
Trevor Phillips
Justin Pollard
Nick Pyne
Catriona Reeves
Jon Riley
Mark Simmons
Colin Simpson
Martin Spiers
Alex Street
Peter Thewlis
Grahame Waite
Brigette Wellbelove
Francis Wheen
Derek Wilson
Valerie Wolf
Lorna Woolfson
Wendalynn Wordsmith